LOVE
is a
LEAP

A TALE ABOUT REINCARNATION
AND A PROMISE MADE

KATE RILEY

ISBN: 978-1-953735-73-7

Published by Satin Romance
An Imprint of Melange Books, LLC
White Bear Lake, MN 55110
www.satinromance.com

Published in the United States of America.

Cover Design by Lynsee Lauritsen

Dedicated to my UK Family—with love, and to my daughters Onion, Gigi and Stinky, who after reading the first chapter, told me that I had to finish it.

With thanks to the team at Melange Books who take my rambling words and turn them into something with polish and purpose. All mistakes made in this book are my own.

LEAP OF FAITH (DEFINITION)

Leap of Faith (definition)
    A **leap of faith**, in its most commonly used meaning, is the act of believing in or accepting something outside the boundaries of reason.

My heart enchanted, has loved you through endless lifetimes before,
and will search for you again, for a hundred lifetimes more.
In life after life, in age after age, I will find you and love you,
from the past, to the present, through lifetimes evermore.

— MICHAEL H. CHAMBERLAIN II, 1868

CHAPTER ONE

*C*lara Irene Bennett was born in the small village of Butleigh, Somerset, to two loving parents who, due to an unfortunate boating accident, promptly died when she was at the tender age of three. This meant that Clara, who was at the time playing with her nanny in her pretty white dress with the little pink roses, was to be raised by her grandfather, Henry Charles Bennett, widower and owner of Bennet's Bookshop, in High Street, Glastonbury. Henry was a kind and gentle man, a bibliophile (as was to be expected by a bookshop owner) and a tad eccentric. And thus, began a childhood that centred around the acquiring of, the reading of, and the selling of, what is popularly known as "new age" books. That and the solid belief in fairies.

Known locally as "Bennet's", the bookshop had been in existence since 1929, when Clara's great-grandfather, James Alexander, seeing the economic prospects of the town's mystical leanings towards antiquarianism, took over a haberdashery shop and transformed the store and himself into a purveyor of books. James, a self-described "aficionado of antiquities", claimed the title with pride and focussed his attention on literary studies. When his son Henry took over the bookshop in 1984, the Glastonbury Festival was already fourteen years old, and with the town's identity being solidly entwined with the Holy Grail, Joseph of Arimathea and King Arthur - continuing the family tradition of alternative books made good economic sense.

The Grade II listed building dates back to the 1700's and retains most of its original rustic charms, with well-worn floorboards that creak, low, oak-beamed ceilings and deep recessed windows that let in just enough light to accent the mood and a promise of what secrets one might find inside. The outside of the building is faithfully whitewashed every twenty years with red painted accents around the windows which set off a heavy, black front door. Last, but by no means least, above the lintel, in bold red Times New Roman lettering, and in pride of place, is "Bennett's Books". However, everyone knows that inside is where the magic really begins. Upon walking through the front door, customers immediately notice the sweet, musky smell of old books that waft into a book-lover's nose, which lingers there teasing the brain. In such a state, new patrons typically stop, take in a deep breath and visibly relax as their busy schedules suddenly take a back seat to the promise of finding something special. Clara knew there was a word for this: *vellichor* – the strange wistfulness of an old bookstore.

The shop is longer in depth than it is in width, with shelves of books, both old and new, lining the walls from top to bottom and front to back. Under the front casement window is a sturdy antique oak table, well-worn with gouges, bumps and scrapes, that currently display her newest books, nestled in a layer of snow-like batting and left-over Christmas decorations of sparkling white snowflakes. Sitting atop a stack of five bestsellers is Clara's favourite chipped ceramic fairy and a sign announcing her post-Christmas special offers.

Midway through the shop is a spiral staircase which leads to the second floor, with a sign at the bottom of the stairs indicating that it is a staff only area. If someone were to venture up these stairs, they would find a surprisingly large space divided into a small office and a loo. The rest of the space is an open area, where several long wooden tables are used for inventory, along with a small kitchenette with an old-fashioned refrigerator which contains a small container of yogurt, a pack of blueberry muffins and some 2% milk. Next to the fridge stands a sink and cupboard, and beside that a laminated table that holds a hot plate, microwave and kettle. Near the balcony is a mismatched, well-used couch and reading chair.

Back on the main floor, towards the rear and off to the side, is a cozy, old dusky-rose chair with stuffing that has seen better days. Beside it is a small side-table, currently stacked with several guidebooks about Glastonbury and just enough room for a cup of tea. On the opposite side are two Deacons benches that Henry Bennett had salvaged from an old church, standing like soldiers against the wall. The books, for the most part, are neatly stacked side-by-side in their assigned sections. Clara, however, prefers to create a more relaxed atmosphere, so customers feel as though they are walking into a private library with literary treasures to be found around every corner. That is why stacks of books are piled up into towers, beside the Deacon benches, next to the comfy chair and on random shelves everywhere. Labels marking the different sections have been neatly printed out, many of them written in her grandfather's hand, and taped to the front of the shelves.

It should come as no surprise that books became a steadying influence in Clara's life. They were always there, never changing. She could read them over and over again and every word remained the same. They didn't die in boating accidents or due to old age. It didn't matter if you lost them or loved them to the point of needing a replacement, the story and characters still remained the same...every single word fixed into place where it always had been. They were predictable and organized. Clara liked that in a book, and in her life.

As a child, Clara had some favourites: Barney Blue-eyes, Black Beauty, Nancy Drew and then later, Mists of Avalon and Philip Pullman's "Dark Materials" series. Having been practically raised in a bookshop, she spent most of her time being polite to customers, learning how to help out, and of course, reading well beyond the age of any of her peers. She devoured all genres, which gave her information that made her knowledgeable. All of this was lovely, but she lacked the practical experiences of life. Friends were few and far between, and even though she knew a few girls that she could consider her friends, she lacked the time and inclination to enjoy herself outside of the bookstore. By the time Clara was a teenager, her grandfather was in his late seventies and needed her help more than ever. This meant that there was no time for boys, or make-up, or flirting, and she was simply too shy to consider going to dances. By the time she was in her mid-twenties, she had inherited the bookshop. So that seemed to be the end, or it would have been, had it not been for Hamish.

Hamish was everything a woman like Clara could ever want. He was handsome enough, tall enough, fit enough, but not so striking that women who were cleverer or prettier than her would ever take notice. His blue-grey eyes were the colour of the skies at Loch Loman and his Scottish accent matched his reddish hair and beard. He was taller than her and his burly physique made her 5'4 figure feel petite. He also had a big laugh. He was handy—especially with the heavy boxes of books that arrived every month for the store. He quite liked to cook and was satisfied by just staying at home with her watching the telly or a movie on the weekend. As an IT consultant, Hamish made good money and was always happy to spend some of it on her. He was, what she would describe as, wonderfully average, which suited her just fine. He had even inherited a Castle—well, the ruins of a castle (with a ghost)—and most importantly, he loved her fervently. The only problem was that Clara was in love with a man who was a product of her own imagination.

Hamish was the main character in Clara's book that she had never had the courage to write. However, this did not deter her. As she saw it, he brought a hopeful joy into her life, and even though she had never met him (as yet), there was the *promise* of him, and that's what kept her going.

Fast-forward ten years, and Clara was still there, reading romance novels, wondering if every man in his mid-thirties who walked through her shop could be *him*. The one who would change her life from ordinary to spectacular. From sale bin to bestseller. But so far, this year's story ending was beginning to look very much like last year, and the year before that; with Clara reading "Pride and Prejudice" on New Year's Eve, eating Chinese food from cardboard boxes and downing a bottle of prosecco, with her cat Lucy for company. But all of this was about to change. What she didn't know that fateful New Year's Eve, was that she was about to embark upon an adventure that no book cover could have hinted at or predicted.

The day started as it always did on 31st of December, with Mrs. Shirley Forde coming by to wish Clara a Happy New Year. The Forde's owned the antique-furniture/psychic reading shop next door, and Mrs. Forde was forever popping by to check on her younger friend. The Forde's were well into their sixties, Mrs. Forde's husband, David, or as he liked to be referred to, Dave, ran the antiques business and took on the odd fix-it job, while his wife, Shirley, did psychic readings when customers requested them. And request them they did. She was quite good at it, with many of her customers hearing about her from word-of-mouth, while her website touted satisfied customer reviews. In terms of the Glastonbury tourist industry, Shirley's psychic readings are considered a "must-experience". Once, when Shirley had given Clara a reading, she confirmed that there would be a Hamish in her life and that she would meet him one day, but not through normal means. She couldn't explain any further, so it was left at that, and that was enough for Clara Bennett.

Upon hearing the bell jingle, Clara looked up from page 35 of "Pride and Prejudice" and smiled. Shirley was bustling her ample body through the bookstore, her face a-flush with excitement, wearing her usual colourful uniform of a tweed skirt, sweater set (various exciting colours) and black stockings. Today's choice was forest green, while her white hair, obviously rinsed with a purple shampoo, gave her a rather festive look. She had in her hand, an old blue leather-bound book.

"Clara! What fun. Come and see what I've found. I thought of you immediately so I had to run over here." Without missing a beat, she continued as she pulled herself a chair. "I finally got around to going through that shipment of estate furniture we received two weeks ago and look what I've found." Handing it to Clara, she pointed out the obvious. "It's an old book."

Clara, by this time, had already bookmarked her own page and had placed "Pride and Prejudice" on the table. Intrigued, she examined the faded and worn blue leather cover and murmured, "Hmm, it is an old one isn't it?"

The title and decorative border on the front were embossed in gold and stated, "A Scientific Inquiry into Metempsychosis" by Professor Michael H. Chamberlain II. However, when she opened the book to what should have been the copywrite page, it was empty. There was no edition, printing information or even a date of publication, although this was sometimes the case with old books, so she wasn't that surprised. The only identifying detail was "Ankh Press MDCCCLXVIII", in tiny letters at the bottom of the page. "Hmmm. The leather may be an indication that it was custom bound for a wealthy reader, and if it's from a wealthy estate that would make sense." Running her fingers across the page she immediately felt the raised type and the quality of the paper. "It feels like rag-based paper. I've never heard of the author, nor the publishing house. Would you like me to see what I can find out and get it evaluated for you?"

"Oh no my dear, you misunderstand. The book is for you. I don't know why, but I have the strongest feeling like it's meant to be yours. Just consider it a book returned to its rightful owner," said Shirley. Then she patted her hand twice on the table as if to confirm her gift and stood up. "I must run back. Are you sure you don't want to come tonight? You'll be missing out on a lot of fun you know."

Clara felt somewhat guilty. Every year she received an invite to share the evening with the Forde's family and as always, she declined. It was very kind of her, but their parties were loud and boisterous, with a particular uncle who, after a few drinks, was a little too friendly come the magic hour of midnight. For Clara, not being with someone special made midnight on New Year's Eve the loneliest moment of the year.

She stood up to give Shirley a hug. "Thank you so much for the gift and thinking of me, Shirley, but no, Lucy and I have a full evening planned."

"Well, if you change your mind, you know where we are. And there's always plenty of food. I'll bring back the folding table and punch bowl we borrowed tomorrow…but not till the afternoon." With a twinkle in her eye, she threw Clara a wink. "It'll take me that long to come down off the chandelier!" As she leaned in for Clara's embrace, she suddenly jumped back as if shocked by a spark of static electricity. She stared hard at Clara for a moment. "You'll be careful tonight, won't you?" Then looking as if she was lost in thought, she slowly walked to the front door, grasped the old iron handle and began to pull it open when she suddenly stopped, looked back at Clara and said, "*Bliadhna Mhath Ùr.*"

Clara's brows knitted in confusion.

Shirley smiled. "It's a wish, a Scottish Happy New Year's wish."

With that she left, leaving Clara standing there, holding on to an old blue leather book wondering whatever had gotten into her friend?

CHAPTER TWO

*C*lara glanced at the book again and out of curiosity, took it over to the computer to search for Michael H. Chamberlain. Nothing. She then tried M. H. Chamberlain, "A Scientific Inquiry into Metempsychosis", still nothing. She tried every variation she could think of, M. H. Chamberlain II, M. H. Chamberlain author, "A Scientific Inquiry into Metempsychosis", Michael H. Chamberlain Professor, Metempsychosis and finally Ankh Press, all of which came to no avail. With Clara's curiosity truly piqued, she typed in metempsychosis. Metempsychosis, she discovered, was the transmigration of the soul of a human being or animal into a new body of the same, or a different, species during death. So, it was essentially a scientific inquiry into reincarnation, which was interesting in itself, but the book and its origins were a complete and utter mystery. Why would Shirley think that this book was meant for her? Frustrated with her lack of information, Clara tucked the book under the counter as some new customers entered the shop.

A handful of tourists came and went, buying the usual guides to Glastonbury and Druid history by various local authors, but by the afternoon there was no walk-in traffic. As the afternoon dragged on, her mind began to wander to happier times. Over in the corner was where she tripped and cut her knee after twirling like a ballerina. Her Grandad had picked her up in his lap, put a plaster on her knee and took her mind off the pain by hunting for fairies. They searched everywhere, under tables, behind books, even inside books, but his favourite method was sitting quietly on the stairs and pretending that he and Clara were invisible. Only then, he told her, would the fairies come out. One had to concentrate and be very quick to even see them; but if you sat still long enough, you'd catch them from the corner of your eye—a glint here, a flash of light there. Clara was always sure that she saw something, and her Grandad never doubted what she saw. After all, what else could it be?

As she sat on the stairs, very still, she looked around and smiled at her own folly for seeing nothing but books and shelves, and long overdue dusting. By 4:00 p.m. it was clear that no other customers would grace her shop, so she turned the door sign to closed and looked around for what needed to be done. The bookshop would be closed for a few days as it was the New Year, so she washed her teacup and ensured the hotplate and kettle were all off before grabbing her favourite hand-woven scarf in delightful blues and greens.

She looked in the mirror as she wrapped her neck in colour, then stopped for a moment to look at her reflection. Clara would never consider herself beautiful, but neither would she consider herself to be ugly. In the right light, her long auburn hair had flecks of red and as of yet, she had no grey hairs that she knew of. Her blue eyes were her strongest feature, and she only knew that because people always commented on them.

Her make-up regime consisted of anything quick, usually some mascara and a dab of blusher, accented by a pair of pearl earrings that had been her mother's. She was neither too skinny, nor too plump, and mostly lived-in blue jeans and sweaters. After all, Hamish loved her just the way she was, so why bother? She took her coat from the stand, put it on and headed for the door. But just as she was about to set the alarm, she remembered the blue book, and retrieved it from under the counter. After popping it into her handbag, she proceeded to lock up.

The drive home to Butleigh didn't take long. As she was driving home, she toyed with the idea of picking up something different to cook for tea, but frozen Chinese was so much easier, and besides, the stores would be busy with last minute shoppers. And she was in no mood to face lengthy queues. Pear Tree Cottage had been her parents' home, and after the accident her grandfather had immediately moved in. It was best, he said, that it be kept for her. After all, it was her inheritance and the only home she had ever known.

Pear Tree was a Grade II listed, thatched cottage, and boasted several period features, including exposed ceiling beams, quarry-tiled floors and wooden windows complete with two picturesque window seats, which were perfect for curling up and reading. Outside was mature gardens with a variety of flowering shrubs and plants, all enclosed around mature hedgerows that afforded the cottage a significant degree of seclusion. It was her own personal castle, and for the next two days, her retreat from the outside world.

After parking her Mini on the drive, Clara fumbled with her keys and entered through the backdoor that led directly into the kitchen. As usual, Lucy loudly greeted her at the door. Clara was never sure whether the three-year-old calico's enthusiasm was more for her or for the fact that she knew she was about to be fed. Considering Lucy's demanding nature, she wouldn't be surprised if it was the latter. Clara then began to make herself a cup of tea as Lucy made figure eights around Clara's ankles until her bowl was finally filled and presented in the usual spot, along with some fresh water in her usual dish. Lucy was very particular that way. She liked to be fed on time, especially in the mornings, closed doors were not permitted, laps were there to be sat on, as were warm computer keyboards, and above all, cuddles before books or there would be consequences. Clara always did her best to comply with Lucy's house rules.

Sitting at the table, she had a sip of her tea and mentally organized her evening: frozen microwave Chinese food, check…prosecco in the fridge, check…cozy pyjamas, snuggly housecoat and woolly socks…check. Fireplace, throw blanket and book all ready to go…check, check and check. The only other thing she could wish for was snow, the big, fat snowflake kind that gently draped her back garden in a soft mantle of white. So why did Clara feel as though something was amiss?

After another sip of her tea, she pictured her copy of "Pride and Prejudice" sitting exactly where she had left it, on the table, back at the shop. Damn. Her first thought was to drive back and get it, but after a quick glance outside she quickly changed her mind as it was snowing! And not just any snow, but big, fat, lacy snowflakes that softly fell on the hedgerows, plants and pear trees. Snow that within an hour would magically transform her garden into a Thomas Kinkade Christmas card. The very picture she had just imagined. "Pride and Prejudice" would just have to wait.

Two hours later she had eaten, changed the sheets on her bed to cozy flannel, changed herself into her favourite nightie with the little red cardinals and pink polar fleece housecoat, thrown a load of laundry into the washer, created a good fire in the wood burner, poured herself a glass of prosecco in one of her mother's crystal wine glasses and opened the curtains so she could enjoy the snowy garden view. Her New Years' Eve was ready to begin. This also happened to be the precise moment she remembered the odd, blue-leather book currently tucked away in her handbag. She returned to the snug after retrieving the tome, and settled into her large easy chair, with her legs tucked under her. As Lucy circled around looking for cozy options, Clara tipped her glass to the feline for a toast, "Happy New Year Lucy" then took a sip of her drink. Lucy responded with a little meow, before moving closer to review a warmer spot nearer the Inglenook.

As she picked up the old book, the first thing she did was close her eyes and inhale the scent of the leather cover. She smiled to herself as she detected aromas of vanilla, dust and almonds; the unforgettable smell of decayed hopes and dreams. As she held onto the book, she began to envision an older man, in an even older leather-worn chair, in a large estate library, who was smoking a pipe…no, a cigar, and was wearing a *"robe de chambre"* of deep blue velvet, ornamented with gold silk frogging and olivettes. What surprised her the most though, was not how vividly he came to mind, nor the certainty that he was smoking a cigar, but that she had no idea what silk frogging or olivettes were. After a quick search on her phone, she managed to answer her own questions. According to the search engine, frog closures are an ornamental closure that typically feature a braided or looped design. Olivettes are spindle-shaped, braided buttons that pass-through frog fastenings. *Perhaps she had read that somewhere?* She then opened the book and once again looked at the copywrite page. Ankh Press, and if her memory served her correctly, MDCCCLXVIII was 1868. Next to the text was the ankh symbol, a teardrop-shaped hoop with a cross connected directly below it, which represented the sun making its path upward and over the horizon. Clara knew that the ankh was an ancient Egyptian symbol which symbolized the many aspects of life, including physical life, eternal life, immortality, death and reincarnation. As she turned to the dedication page, her heart skipped a beat.

> *To Klara,*
> *My heart enchanted, has loved you through endless lifetimes before,*
> *and will search for you again, for a hundred lifetimes more.*
> *In life after life, in age after age, I will find you and love you,*
> *from the past, to the present, through lifetimes evermore.*

Slightly shaken, she took a large sip of prosecco, and then another one for good measure. Shirley had said she was returning the book to its rightful owner, but the book was written in 1868. Clara was an old-fashioned name, and certainly popular in the 1860's, so obviously it was a coincidence. Maybe Shirley had seen the dedication? But why could Clara imagine the man in the smoking jacket so clearly? Looking outside she watched the snow falling as she continued to think about the poem, then drained the last of her glass. What if the poem really *was* meant for her? Refilling her wine glass, she read the poem aloud, slowly, as if each word was a magical incantation... *In life after life, in age after age, I will find you and love you, from the past, to the present, through lifetimes evermore.* Could such a love exist?

Turning the page, Clara began to read the rest of the book, but unfortunately Lucy had other plans. Jumping onto her lap the cat proceeded to make her wishes known in regards to wanting Clara's undivided attention by rubbing her head on the edge of the book, which made reading impossible. At first, Clara scratched Lucy behind the ears and attempted to lure her into her lap to sleep, but Lucy was having none of it. She was insistent and demanding, her message was clear. Put the book down and pay attention to me, right now! Frustrated, Clara tried to shoo her off, but Lucy was determined and knew her mistress well. What was needed here was a little retaliatory action. As she leapt off Clara's lap and onto the floor, Lucy casually walked over to the side table next to the bookcase and proceeded to jump onto a shelf containing Clara's collection of treasured antiques acquired by her parents. This of course mattered not one wit to Lucy, who looked once at Clara and then batted the first object her paw could connect with.

Now, the concept of Murphy's Law is as old as humanity, and the perversity of the universe has been long discussed, but to state it simply: Anything that can go wrong will go wrong, just as it did this New Year's Eve for Clara Irene Bennett. In fact, the chain of events that happened next, would change Clara's life forever.

First of all, a small china piece came flying off the shelf and landed at Clara's feet. She was not impressed; but as she scolded

Lucy and told her to get off the shelf, the mantelpiece loosened its moorings from the wall and everything tumbled to the floor in a heap of crystal, china and a calico cat, that howled and escaped into another room before she could catch her.

Clara held her breath. This. Was. Supposed. To. Be. A. Quiet. New. Year's. Eve! Instead, it was a disaster zone, and she was livid!

Jumping up from her chair she surveyed the damage, took another large gulp of prosecco and swore for the second time that evening. "Bugger!"

The second thing that happened, was that after jumping up from her chair, taking a swig of prosecco and yelling "Bugger", she took a step forward to survey the damage, stepped on a piece of broken china, causing her to fall backwards, lose her balance and hit her head on the corner of the coffee table, knocking herself unconscious.

The third thing, and most importantly what Clara could never have predicted, was that she woke up in the 17th Century.

A LOVER'S LEAP

*C*lara lay there with her eyes closed, focusing on the throbbing pain from the bump on her head. A chilly breeze brushed her cheek, and the strong scent of snow, damp earth and meadow awakened her senses that something significant had just happened. Her head felt fuzzy, and she felt displaced, as if she was in two places at once. *Where was she?* A man called out a name she recognized as hers, but not "Clara", something else…something familiar, but lost in time. His voice boomed with a thick Scottish accent and the vibrations of heavy hooves thundered towards her. In an instant someone was by her side. "Dorothea, are you all right?"

Clara opened her eyes to the most handsome man she had ever seen, his eyes riveted to hers in deep concern. His reddish-brown hair was shoulder-length and hung in tangled, wild curls, framing a strong jawline and deep brown eyes that drew her to him: they drew her into his world, and Clara, feeling herself pulled into someone named Dorothea, went willingly, knowing in her soul that she already knew him, that she already loved him, that she desperately needed to see him again.

Little puffs of his warm breath escaped into the chilled air as he anxiously searched her face. "Dorothea, speak to me. Are you alright love?"

"Yes, but I've bumped my head. For a second there, I felt strange, like I was two people."

"I'm not surprised, that was a nasty fall, and the ground is hard this time of year." Placing one hand behind her neck, he gently helped her into a sitting position. "Slowly, slowly now. Let me have a look."

The hand-spun coat he was wearing tightened around his muscled arms and she drank in his musky scent. As he leaned in closer, she could feel his warm breath against her skin and her mind wandered like it always did when he was near.

"You'll have a nasty bump on that pretty head of yours. Can you move your limbs? Have you broken anything?"

"No, Hamish, I'm fine." Irritated because he had broken the spell, she added. "You worry too much."

"Damn you, woman, you scared the hell out of me! I should never have allowed you to ride Champion."

"Allowed me? You forget yourself, sir. You may be my very best friend in the world, but you're hardly in a position to not allow me to do anything."

"I am very well aware, m'lady that I am merely a servant in the grand Dunbrae Castle, but you cannot stop me from worrying about you."

Mercurial as usual, she snapped back. "Don't ever say that Hamish. You know you're more than a servant to me and always will be. If things were different…"

He smiled at her gently and his voice was soft. "What Thea…? You'd run away with me? Be my wife and share my bed? Be happy in a little thatched cottage with a dozen bairns underfoot?"

She slapped his arm. "Well maybe not a dozen, ye' daft idiot."

"Fair enough, I suppose, but sadly lass, that's not our lot is it. Maybe in another life but not in this one."

Dorothea lowered her eyes and smiled. "I'll hold you to that Hamish McLure, so I will."

"As will I, Dorothea of Dunbrae. As will I. Come on, let's see if you can stand up and I'll help you up on Lorcan. Your father will have my head if I've broken his daughter."

Taking a hold of her arm, he helped her to her feet and then walked a few steps with her before he was confident that she hadn't seriously hurt herself.

As Hamish strode over to retrieve his horse who nibbled away on a patch of dried grass, Thea brushed off the loose snow and debris from her skirt. When he returned, she did a little twirl. "How do I look?"

"Like the Earl of Dunsmore's beautiful daughter who rides too fast for her own good." Leaning over, he locked his fingers together to form a step. He nodded towards the horse. "Now, get up on Lorcan so I can walk you back to the castle like a proper lady."

Once she was seated, Hamish took two steps back, lowered his knee and extended his arm in a slow exaggerated bow. She looked down at his smiling face. "Go on with ye, Hamish McLure, you know me too well for that nonsense." And with that she booted the horse's flanks, leaving him standing alone in the meadow thinking how a man like him would sell his soul for a marvelous woman like that.

∼

She had no sooner arrived back in her room when her maidservant Bessie rushed into her chamber and began to fuss about. A ruddy-cheeked, full-bosomed lass with an ample figure, her hands were fluttering with anxiety. "Quick, m'lady, you need to change. Your mother wants you in her chambers now, and I don't ken she's in the mind to wait."

Dorothea rolled her eyes and exhaled a deep sigh. "She's never in the mind to wait, Bessie. What is it now?"

"I'm sure I don't know, m'lady, but cook says there's a good dinner tonight. Perhaps it's to do with a guest, or what dress she wants you to wear."

"As well as what to say to whom and when. You can be certain of that." Putting her arms out to her sides to better enable Bessie to dress her, she scowled. "Let's get on with it." As Bessie helped her into her kirtle, she knitted her brows in a little arch. "It's odd that we are having guests so close to Hogmanay. Are you quite sure you don't know what it's about?"

"I don't, I swear, m'lady, but downstairs, they're talking about a possible suitor."

"A suitor? Whatever for?"

"So, you can be married to a fine gentleman, m'lady."

"Bessie, I have already thought long and well of this matter and I have several considerations before I will be happy with a husband. The most important of these is that he must love me, and I love him. Who is this would-be suitor?"

Bessie looked up at her mistress then lowered her eyes and whispered. "The Marquess, m'lady."

Dorothea began to laugh. "You can't be serious, Bessie. His head is all feather inside and out, and he talks of nothing but dances and duals. The man is older than God and besides I'm sure even you have heard the rumours of his 'preferences'. Whatever would he want with a young woman of seventeen?"

Bessie opened her mouth to speak, but it was her mother's clipped voice who answered. Erect of gait, her green watered-silk dress swished loudly as she strode into her daughter's chamber. With her nose in the air, she looked her daughter up and down and replied with authority. "It's very simple, Dorothea. He wants an heir so that when he dies, he can leave his estate to his son and wife and that, my dear, will be you. And because, as you so cleverly point out, he is older than God, this means it won't be that far off. Simply bear him a child and your future will be set, as will be the future of Dunbrae."

Dorothea's face drained with shock. "Surely you can't be serious, Mama."

"Thea, you are of age and you can't possibly think that we would ever allow you to marry a servant." As her daughter lowered her eyes and blushed, she carried on. "Don't think I haven't noticed your growing infatuation. It's time to put away childish things and begin your duties as a woman to this family. The sooner the better. Your father and I are in accord that this is an excellent opportunity for you, as well as a suitable match. After you have married His Lordship and borne him a son, you can dally wherever you want. Until then, I suggest you carry yourself with the utmost decorum as befitting the future bride of a Marquess."

Thea stamped her foot. Her eyes flashed fire. "I won't do it, Mama. I refuse."

"I'm afraid that's not possible, Thea. Your father and I have already approved the match and your bridegroom will be dining with us this evening when your engagement will be announced. You'll be married by Hogmanay."

Slowly walking around her daughter in a circle, she was thoughtful for a moment, then spoke directly to Bessie. "Your Ladyship will wear the white satin tonight with the pink panelled sleeves and matching petticoat. I suggest the pearl eardrops and pearl necklace. You'll do her hair up in curls. It will make her look a little more mature."

Bessie nodded that she understood and with a quick curtsey excused herself, to prepare her mistress.

Dorothea's face was deep red with frustration, and she had tears in her eyes. "You can't expect me to go through with this. I...I...would have to be intimate with him, Mama."

Lady Dunsmore simply rolled her eyes and sighed. "Oh, Thea, don't be so dramatic! You act as if everyone married for love. The sooner you acquaint yourself with how the world works the better." With that, she tilted her chin up and turned to leave.

"Once you are mistress of your own household, with children of your own, you will understand better how things are. Until then, your duty is to obey. I will see you at dinner. And Thea, my dear, do try and look pleasant."

CHAPTER FOUR

*T*hea stood in front of her mirror and eyed the young woman reflected before her. Dressed in the satin gown her mother had demanded that she wear, she knew she looked beautiful but inside, she felt dead. She was a young woman whose life had ended at seventeen.

Bessie reviewed her handiwork from the side. "You look beautiful, m'lady, but I think you need a little something extra for your hair. You've got quite the bump on your head from that fall, so I've left that area a little looser." Thinking for a moment, her eyes widened, and her face beamed with a smile. "I know just the thing. I'll be back in a moment. I'm going to fetch some wee seed pearls. We'll circle them around so your mother will be none the wiser."

Continuing to stare into the mirror, Thea looked behind her reflection towards the casement window where the late afternoon December sun cast the last of its long beams on the oaken floor. Turning she walked towards the light and with a heavy heart looked out the window. The sun, now a glorious burst of deep golden-orange was slowing sinking on the horizon into a sky of darkening blue. In minutes it would be gone, just like her childhood was about to be. She always knew that one day she would have to leave her home and everything familiar to her, but this was too soon. She wasn't ready, and as far as she was concerned, it wasn't fair.

Looking out at the castle's stonework she tried to remember what her father had explained to her. Although Dunbrae appeared to be one building, it was actually two towers joined together.

The original castle had started out as a large three-storey building, with a small garret under the roof. In her great-grandfather's time though, he had added a much larger L-shaped second tower. Built alongside the original building there was a six-foot gap between them. The second tower was connected to the newer tower by a wooden bridge below the level of the battlements. Built for defensive reasons, it was thought that if one tower was attacked the residents could then flee into the second and draw up the bridge between the two. The newer and more spacious tower was now used by the family, while the older original part of the castle was used to quarter the servants.

Lost in thought, she didn't notice Hamish from the window in the opposite tower until he softly called out her name. "Thea."

Turning to follow his voice, their eyes locked, and a single smile spoke what each of them knew to be true in their hearts. Words that they dare not speak or commit to yet was understood all the same. They loved each other body and soul.

"You look beautiful."

Thea looked down at her finery and felt helpless. What she wouldn't give to have done all of this for his benefit alone. Looking back at him, she then lowered her eyes and smiled. "Thank you, Hamish."

"It's not your fault, but my heart is broken, Thea."

Barely above a whisper, she replied, "And my own, Hamish... and my own."

～

Elegantly dressed in his blue velvet coat, brocade waistcoat and breeches, her father took her arm as she descended the stairs.

"I ken you're not thrilled with our choice, Dorothea, but you'll get over it quick enough when you've got wee ones t' chase after and a large house to manage." Giving her a once over, he nodded in approval. "You're doin' me proud tonight, lass."

Thea managed a small smile, noting that he was wearing his best periwig, the one that cascaded in perfect curls down his back, a sure sign that he meant not only to impress but also how committed he was to the business arrangement.

A modest assembly of family and friends stood about quietly chatting, then suddenly stopped as they entered the hall, while a smaller party that included her mother and the Marquess turned and looked her way. All eyes were upon her. As her father escorted her forward, her mother nodded her approval, then quickly glanced to the Marquess in an evident attempt to assess his reaction to her daughter's entrance. Clearly from the lecherous smile on his face he approved.

Thea looked at her future husband standing before her and silently screamed inside. Dressed in a bright red velvet topcoat with elegant gold trim and accents, his deep blue brocade waistcoat underneath fitted snugly against a belly that obviously consumed a lot of ale. Around his neck hung a white lace ascot that completed his fashionable ensemble in a probable effort to contain his sagging jowls. His periwig, in a similar style to her father's, was in a reddish hue and cascaded curls down the front of his coat. Arrogance and money. To Dorothea, despite his outward finery he was simply a disgusting old man who had just bought a prize filly. She felt physically sick to her stomach and it was all she could do to manage a smile.

At that moment, the Chamberlain announced dinner, to which her father took her mother's arm, leaving the Marquess to extend his to Thea's.

His reedy voice grated in her head. "May I escort you to your seat?"

A pleasant reply refused to come from her lips so she did her best to just smile and nod. What else could she do? She felt like she was trapped in a bad dream as they walked through into the Grand Hall where an enormous linen-draped table was lavishly decorated with their best silver candlesticks, platters, salt cellars, plates, cutlery and goblets. Everything was on display for the Marquis' benefit—especially her.

It was no surprise that she was then seated beside the Marquess who after settling his large frame, nodded politely to her before taking a large swig of wine. Looking around the table, the inevitability of it all was further brought home by the sneer of her cousin who had already been married off the year before in a similar situation. Feeling cowed into obedience, she lowered her eyes and willed herself not to cry.

Dinner was a blur of stern looks from her mother to smile, polite talk, and innuendoes from the Marquess that made her cheeks blush. How would she ever get out of this? The man had passed enough wind to kill a woodcock and enough wine that his bulbous nose was flushed red with drink. He was in a word, repulsive. Lost in thought, she didn't catch what had been said, nor what was apparently being toasted to, as her father rose from his seat. Raising his glass in the air, he gave a nod to His Lordship and then to her.

"A toast to His Lordship and to my lovely daughter." With that, everyone stood and drank to their future happiness.

The Marquess then stood and faced Dorothea. Fumbling to retrieve something from his waist pocket he held out a silver broach to show everyone. "As a token to my beloved, I give this *luckenbooth* to you, to show my good faith." Taking her hand, he raised it to his lips.

She tried to focus but couldn't. Her head pounded. There was a loud buzzing in her ears, and she felt nauseous. The room became very hot and began to spin. Suddenly there was the sensation of bodies at her side, her mother's voice... "Overcome by love your Grace." Then darkness.

CHAPTER FIVE

*D*orothea awoke in her bed but had no sense of time or how she had got there. As she started to stir, Bessie's concerned face hovered above hers. "How are you feeling, m'lady?"

"Where am I?"

"You're in your chambers, m'lady."

Thea knitted her brows and attempted to raise her head but gave up. "What...what happened?"

"Ye fainted, m'lady, is all. At least that's what the doctor said, but he did notice that nasty bump on your head. I didn't say a word how you got it, honest I didn't, but I don't mind sayin', I was mighty worried at how long you slept."

"Oh, God, I remember now. He..." She stopped, her eyes darting around to see if anyone else was in the room. "What time is it?"

"It's okay, it's just us two here now and it's morning, ma'am."

Thea grabbed Bessie's hand and locked eyes with her maid-servant's. "It was too much, Bessie. I just remember feeling revolted. It was all too much, then suddenly the room was spinning. Was Mama angry?"

"I heard she wasn't pleased, m'lady, but the headman Martin, told me that the Marquess didn't seemed bothered either way. He just kept drinkin' and carrying on as if nothing had happened."

Crestfallen, Thea put her hands to her face. "What am I supposed to do, Bessie?"

The swishing of her mother's silk skirts alerted Bessie, who rose from her mistress's side and speaking in a louder voice than she needed to, said, "I'll go and fetch your mother, m'lady. I ken she'll be pleased to know that you're feeling better."

No sooner had she turned around when Lady Dunsmore walked in. Her pale face was a good indication that she had drank too much claret herself.

"I see, daughter, that you are awake. Good."

Taking the lead from Bessie who seemed to have anticipated her mother's mood, she quietly apologized. "I'm sorry, Mama, I don't know what came over me."

"I'm sure you are, but you'll be happy to know that all is well, and they'll be crying the banns in church tomorrow. It will be a New Year's wedding so there's only days to prepare."

"Hogmanay!"

"Yes. You shouldn't be surprised. We were already planning a grand affair so there's no need to wait." Touching her hand to her hair, she continued. "Imagine, my daughter a Marquess. That's quite the honour for your father and I!"

Her head hurt and she felt broken. "Yes, Mama."

"Oh, there's one more thing, Thea. Dr. Morris said you had a bump on your head and suggested that it may have been caused by a fall from your horse. Is this true?"

Thea pursed her lips and sighed. "I took a small tumble yesterday, Mama but it was my own fault."

"And when you took this small tumble, Thea, were you with the groomsman Hamish?"

Knowing where this was headed, Thea shook her head. "No, Mama. I swear I took Champion out on my own and against his recommendation."

"I see. And he knew none of this?"

"No, Mama."

"Well, I suppose he has enough good sense for that. I'll inform your father as such. From now on, Dorothea, I forbid you to ride without an escort of *my choosing*, to ensure you ride at a pace that suits a lady, not a head-strung young girl. You can be assured that it will not be Hamish." She put up her hand as Thea opened her mouth. "Before you argue, Dorothea, I assure you that I am doing this for his sake as well. Your father would be very disappointed if his best horseman was involved in your childish whims."

Thea closed her eyes and sighed. "Yes, Mama."

"Excellent. I'm glad we have an understanding. Now, I need you out of this bed, dressed and in my chambers. We have a wedding to plan."

∼

After her mother had left, Bessie shyly stepped forward in order to help her mistress out of her bed, but in a fit of frustration Thea pulled the covers over her head, kicked her feet and screamed. "I won't do it!"

Bessie sat on the side of the bed and offered her sympathy. "I'm so sorry for your disappointment, but I don't ken how you'll get out of this, m'lady."

"I'll run away."

"And live on what?"

"Hamish will provide for me."

Alarmed, Bessie asked, "Does Hamish know about this?"

"Of course not, Bessie, nor would he agree to it. He has too much honour. You know that."

"Even so, m'lady, best not repeat it again. You'll get him in more trouble than he already is."

"Why? What trouble is he in?"

"Not so much trouble, m'lady, but it's hardly a secret how he feels about you. Forgive me, for sayin' but if you weren't the Earl of Dunsmore's daughter, you'd already be wedded and bedded, I can assure you of that."

Thea's heart fluttered as she looked up at Bessie and smiled. Blushing, she whispered, "I know." And it was in that exact moment, she knew what she must do.

The plan was a simple one. She would have her wedding night, but it wouldn't be with the Marquess. Before dooming herself to a loveless marriage, she would experience true love to the fullest and experience enough passion to last her a lifetime. The problem was where and when, and more importantly, convincing Bessie to help.

As Thea rose out of bed, Bessie opened the drapes wide to let in the light, causing her to wince. "Bessie, I've still got a tinge of a headache. Can you close the drapes a wee bit?"

"Of course, I can, m'lady." Darkening the room just a touch, she turned back and reviewed what needed to be done. "Would you prefer the blue or brown today, Ma'am?"

"I think the blue dress will be fine for today, but before you go, I want to speak with you. I need you to do something for me, Bessie. Something important, and if you agree I'll make sure that you come with me as my lady's maid when I marry the Marquess."

"Is this anything to do with Hamish, m'lady? Because I could be let go if anyone found out and I've nowhere else t' go."

"I know, which is why we must agree on secrecy. No one must find out. We would both be ruined."

Bessie fidgeted with the ends of her hair for a moment while she twisted her lips in thought. Finally, she gave her answer. "What do you need me t' do?"

Thea, who had been holding her breath, let out a large sigh. "Thank you. Thank you. Bessie, I will never forget this kindness. I need you to give him a letter for me and then I'll need you to make sure we are alone tonight. Do you understand what I'm asking?"

"I believe I do, m'lady."

Thea blushed and lowered her eyes. "I'm sorry, Bessie, but I have no one else to ask. I have to ask an indelicate question... Have you...?"

Bessie blushed as well, and quickly looked away. "I have, m'lady, and you've no need to worry on that account. Hamish is a tender-hearted man and I have no reason to believe he won't be kind to you. Everyone is nervous on the first time and he'll understand that."

Thea listened carefully, then nodded her head.

Bessie drew a deep breath. "I beg your pardon though, m'lady, why would you risk doing this, three days before your wedding?"

"I would rather have the man I love be the first to touch me, Bessie, you must understand that."

"I do, m'lady, but what if he says he can't come to you tonight?"

"He will. He'll have already heard what happened last night and I need to see him. Besides, he'll worry when he's heard that I fainted."

"But what if he gets you with child?"

Dorothea held her head up and looked at her maid eye-to-eye. "I'm counting on it."

CHAPTER SIX

Thea had spent the better part of the day in her mother's chambers pretending to be resigned to her fate, but all the while attempting to calm the butterflies in her stomach. For her part, Bessie had confirmed the rendezvous with a single nod as she held various fabrics up against her mistress's face. Thea blushed. Tonight, she would hold Hamish in her arms and freely give herself to him with all the love and devotion of a new bride. She flushed at the thought of it.

After having to repeat herself twice, her mother looked at her daughter with concern. "Dorothea, are you all right? I've asked you twice about the silk brocade and you haven't heard a word I've said."

"I'm sorry, Mama, it's just that I'm tired after last night. In fact, I still have a twinge of a headache."

"Hmmm. Perhaps we should ask Dr. Morris to come by. He can give you a tincture of something to help you sleep."

"No, Mama, I'm fine. I'm sure if I retire early, I'll be feeling much better in the morning."

"It's probably all the excitement. After all, it's not every day that we welcome a Marquess into the family. Bessie can bring something light up for you to eat."

"Thank you, Mama. I'm certain I'll be as fit as a fiddle by tomorrow and ready to continue with the preparations."

"Very well then. Give your mama a kiss and off you go. Mind you get a good night's sleep."

As they climbed the stairs to her chamber, Thea began to whisper, but Bessie widened her eyes and put a finger to her lips, as Bessie was quite aware of how easily gossip spread through the household.

When they were certain they were alone, Thea's face brightened. "Tell me everything, Bessie. What did he say when he read the note?"

"He smiled, nodded, and said to tell you he would be here."

"That's it?"

"Well, he's hardly going to say anything to me, now is he? I've given him the skirt like you asked, so no one will know it's not me and we'll get him out before dawn the same way."

Thea embraced her maid in a hug. "Bessie, thank you so much. I promise you'll never regret this."

Surprised, Bessie awkwardly hugged her back, doing her best to hold back her tears. Then, retrieving the note from the folds of her dress, she threw it into the fire. "Now let's get you presentable, shall we?"

As the evening wore on, Thea thought she would die of waiting. Would he show up? What if he was caught? What if he changed his mind? She tried reading to quiet down her mind, but after only a few pages she couldn't go on. The weather outside was turning foul and she could hear the whistling of the wind against the windowpane. The room had been prepared with enough logs to last the night. A large sheep's skin had been laid in front of the hearth and a carafe of her father's best claret had been poured in advance, along with two goblets. Cold meats, bread and a wedge of cheese had been laid out. A detail that Bessie assured her would be appreciated. All that was missing was the groom.

Bessie had gone out to meet Hamish where they had agreed, and to give him her scarf. If everything went well, he should be here by now. In that very moment came a quiet knock on her chamber door.

Rushing to open it, she blushed, smiled and took his hand. "You're here."

Behind him stood Bessie, who gave a quick smile and a nod. "I'll be here should you need me, m'lady."

Stepping into her chamber, Hamish looked back at her spell-bound. She was wearing a loose blue brocaded mantua over a shift that more than hinted of her naked body underneath. Bessie had loosened her auburn hair and brushed it until it shone. It now fell in long loose curls down her back and across her breasts.

Taking her hand, Hamish held it to his lips. "Are you all right, Thea? I heard you fainted last night. After that tumble you took, I was worried."

Taking his other hand in hers, she smiled then walked him further into the room and handed him a goblet of claret. He was dressed in a clean linen shirt and leather vest. His hose showing off his shapely, well-muscled thighs.

"I'm much better now. I had to see you, Hamish. I had to see you before, before they marry me off to that hideous old man."

Overcome, she began to cry as he pulled her close and enfolded her into his manly arms. He closed his eyes and kissed her head. "There, there Thea. It's all right, love."

Lost in his embrace, she smelled the musk of him and the want of being nowhere else but here in his arms. "I wanted my first time to be with the man I love, Hamish. I want it to be with you."

"Ah, lass, you're a rare one." He looked at her with a smirk.

"What are you smiling at?"

He chuckled back at her. "Before you have your wanton way with me, and before I love you enough to ruin you for any other man, will you first accept a token of my love? I wouldn't want you t' think I'm not an honorable man."

"I would never think that, Hamish. You must know that."

"I do, but still. I'd like things to be proper between us." From his vest pocket, he pulled out a simple small silver locket crafted into a heart and placed it in her hand. "It's only a wee thing I know and not near what you deserve, but I wanted you to have it."

Thea looked lovingly into his eyes and raising her lips to his, she whispered, "I do." Then, suddenly overcome with shyness, she lowered her head and blushed.

Hamish took her into his arms and lifted her chin so that she could feel his ragged breath against hers. "I do too. Now kiss me woman before I die from wanting you."

Deftly picking her up in his muscled arms, he carried her over to the hearth and gently lowered her onto the sheepskin rug. Laying on his side beside her, he lovingly gazed at her, then ran his fingers through her hair. "You're the most beautiful woman I ever seen." Then leaned over and kissed her slowly.

Thea felt as if she was drowning and never wanted to surface for air again. His kiss was deep, and as she fell, she lost herself fully into his embrace. Wanting more, she matched his passion until both surfaced gasping for air. Hamish's breath was rapid, and his hands shook. "You're sure about this, Thea? If you've changed your mind, you need to tell me now, because I don't know if I'll be able to stop myself."

Thea was breathing heavily herself and even though she was nervous, she had never been surer of anything else in her life. "I don't ever want you to stop."

His hands were shaking as he slowly undid her gown and as she sat up to pull her shift over her head, he threw his vest and shirt to the side. Standing now, he pulled down his breeches revealing his erect manhood. Taking a quick look at Thea, he took a goblet of wine and handed it to her, taking the other for himself. Entwining their arms together each took a long sip. "In front of God I take you as my betrothed, Dorothea Dunsmore, and so help me God, I'll never love another."

Thea raised her goblet and said, "In front of God I take you as my betrothed, Hamish McLure, and so help me God, I'll love only you."

Finishing off the wine they hungrily fell together. He entered her gently, repeatedly asking if she was okay, but she was too far gone now, lost in her body being an extension of him. With each thrust she wanted, needed him to go deeper. Their rhythm was sometimes frantic, and sometimes slow. His mouth on her breast filled her with a desperate burst of passion she could barely contain. Opening herself up, body and soul, she willingly let him swallow her whole. They were as one.

The following morning, she was awakened by the sound of Bessie calling her from a deep dreamy sleep. "M'lady, your mother is asking after you and it's late, what do you want me to say."

Thea raised herself on one arm and looked beside her. Seeing the other side empty, she felt an odd combination of sadness and relief. "Where's Hamish?"

"I woke him early, m'lady. He was away with no issue at all."

"How was he? Was he…happy?"

"Like a man after his wedding night." Bessie smiled. "So, m'lady, you're a full-on woman now. Was it everything you'd hoped it would be?"

Thea was beaming. "Oh, Bessie, I feel like I could burst with happiness."

"Well, you'd better be a wee *less* happy if your t' spend the day with your mother."

Flopping her arm against her forehead she groaned. "Oh God, I forgot."

"There's two days to your wedding, m'lady. Let's start you off with a scrub before you meet with her Ladyship. From the smell of you, it wouldn't be hard to ken what you've been doing."

Thea simply responded with a blissful smile.

As the day wore on, she became increasingly tired and cross

with all the decisions she was expected to be participating in. Truthfully, she couldn't have cared less and was happy for her mother to take over everything. A service her mother was more than happy to provide. The small headache she had yesterday had not left her.

Tomorrow would be the last day before her wedding that she would be able to see Hamish.

CHAPTER SEVEN

$\mathcal{J}$t was the evening of the 31st of December 1638, the night before her marriage to the Marquess and Thea was hell-bent on seeing Hamish one last time. Once again, she had enlisted Bessie's help, who swore up and down to her mistress that this would be the very last time. Her servant did everything she could to make her see reason. The cost of being found out was too great. Hamish could be killed. She would be sacked. But nothing could stop her from seeing him one last time.

Her headache had become more pronounced over the day, making her short as she exchanged clothes with Bessie. Wrapping her servant's worn brown scarf around her she hurried down the stairs and into the night. Once she reached the servant's tower, she cowered next to the stairs as an exhausted kitchen maid who didn't even give her a second look plodded her way to the female quarters towards the back. A little unnerved, she stood still and waited until she was certain that no one else was around. She then quietly climbed the stone stairway all the way to the top to Hamish's small garret and tapped on his door. Hamish swung the door open, his mouth dropping when he realized who it was. Quickly bundling her inside, he firmly shut the door. "Thea, what are you doing here?"

She took in his room. A cot barely long enough to fit his long legs was covered with a thin quilt. A single candle sitting on a small make-shift table lit the tiny room. "I had to see you one last time Hamish."

He held her tightly, then pressed his face into her hair. "I know. I couldn't stop thinking of you all day. I thought I'd go mad with the want of you."

Shivering, she leaned into the warmth of his strong arms and kissed his cheek. "I know I shouldn't have come but I couldn't help myself. I had to see you."

"Shhh, lass. Come lay here with me for a while." Hamish lay on his side with his back to the wall in order to keep her as warm as possible. They spooned together as he held her close and kissed the back of her head.

She sighed blissfully. "Promise we'll be together one day, Hamish."

"I promise, love. If not in this lifetime, the one after that or the one after that."

Thea smiled. "And how will I recognize you?"

"By my handsome good looks of course."

She giggled then snuggled in closer. "Is that a fact, and how will you recognize me?"

"That's easy, by the fire in your eyes and the love in your heart. And that mark on the back of your shoulder blade."

Thea half turned and grinned. "Hamish McLure, I have no such thing."

"Oh, you do wife, you do indeed. And it's the prettiest, sweetest mark I've ever seen. It looks just like the heart I gave you."

"Go away with you, Hamish."

Suddenly there was an urgent knock on the door. Jumping up from the bed, Hamish opened the door a crack to reveal Bessie in an extreme state of agitation. "M'lady, your mother is on her way here. We're in a real state if she sees you. I wouldn't open your chamber door and I pretended I was you like you asked, but I could hear that she didn't believe me. She's on her way here. I slipped out the backway and took the bridge, but she'll be here soon. You've got to leave now, m'lady."

Thea was now standing beside Hamish but before she could open her mouth, they heard a commotion below.

Hamish, spoke to Bessie first. "Go back to your Lady's chamber the way you came and wait for her there."

Thea added her own order. "And open my shutters. Run!" Bessie didn't need to be told twice.

Turning back to Thea he was shocked to see her in front of the casement window, his own shutters ajar. "What are you doing? Surely you don't mean to jump?"

"There's no time, Hamish. Help me up."

"Thea, I can't let you do this."

"And I can't allow you to stop me, Hamish. Just remember your promise."

On the outside ledge she made her way to the roof top edge where he watched transfixed in horror at her intention to jump across to the other tower. He couldn't breathe. Then, suddenly, with one mighty leap she achieved the impossible. Safely on the other tower she clambered through her now open bedroom window. Hamish had just enough time to catch his breath and bolt the window before his chamber door was kicked open.

Still puffing from running, Bessie helped Thea as she scrambled through the window and tumbled to the floor. "Quick, Bessie, help me to my bed." Squeezing her eyes shut she put her hand to her head and winced.

Wide-eyed the servant put her hand to her chest. "Oh my God, m'lady, have y' hurt yourself?"

"No, it's this headache, Bessie, it's so much worse."

"Here, let me help you into bed and in a minute, I'll get you some warm milk. You've had quite the adventure, m'lady. I canna believe you jumped that far."

With barely enough time to cover Thea, her Ladyship returned. This time though, she opened the door immediately when requested.

"Why was the door locked?"

Thea answered weakly. "It's not Bessie's fault. I asked her to Mama."

She tried to raise her head but couldn't. "I'm not feeling well."

Walking over to the bed, she looked at her daughter's pale face and worry instantly replaced her anger. Something was clearly wrong.

"Bessie, we need Dr. Morris now. Get a guard to fetch him immediately."

Bessie took a quick fearful look at Thea and hurried to the door. "Yes, ma'am."

And so, it was, that on New Year's Eve 1638, as the rest of the castle prepared for a wedding celebration and Hamish lay on his bed thinking of his love, Bessie frantically yelled orders for a guard to fetch the doctor, the Earl of Dunsmore raced to his daughter's chambers and Dorothea's mother sat on her daughter's bed holding her limp and clammy hand.

Thea's head was splitting in two, the room spinning out of control. There was a sense of still being in her body, one moment with excruciating pain, and then the other with shards of light and glimmers of peace.

Her mother was speaking, but as if from a distance. The stars sweetly beckoned, and she followed willingly. The edges of her chamber began to turn dark and as the final flickers of firelight danced shadows under her eyelids, she felt herself slipping away, somewhere far, to another time and place. Somewhere in the future where a promise was being kept.

a woman's voice rang out from the darkness. "Clara! Clara, my dear, are you all right, sweetheart?"

Her head ached, and as she reached behind to touch the pain, she realised someone had asked her a question. "Bessie?" *Was that her voice?*

"Bessie? No, dear, it's Shirley. Are you all right love?"

Confused, Clara slowly opened her eyes to see Bessie's face hovering above her. But not Bessie. It seemed to be a version of Bessie, but a much older version of her with lilac hair and a chubbier face. *Just how long had she fainted? Where was she?*

"Where's...Hamish?"

"You're confused, dear. There's no Hamish here."

Memories swirled around, mixed all together like a whirlpool of colours. "Where am I?"

"You're at home, love. It's Shirley."

"Shirley." She repeated it for the familiarity of the name. "Shirley."

"That's right. And do you know who you are?"

"Thea...no, no that's not right, is it? I'm Clara now, aren't I?"

"Yes dear, that's right." Shirley leaned forward and with an encouraging smile, put one hand under her neck and held her hand with the other. "Now let's see if you can sit up. It looks like you've got a nasty gash there that may need some stitches."

Clara, still a little dizzy, winced and closed her eyes so they would adjust, as Shirley gently lifted her up into a sitting position. Still kneeling beside her, Shirley held her tight. "You, all right?"

"Yes, just give me a minute."

Slowly opening her eyes again, she looked around at her surroundings. She was expecting to see a castle chamber, but little by little she returned to being Clara and in her home. "What day is it?"

"It's 1st January, New Year's Day dear. What day did you think it was?"

Clara knitted her brows. "My wedding day… But that's not possible is it?" Suddenly it dawned on her and she smiled! With a huge rush of relief, she grabbed Shirley's arm and exclaimed, "I'm not married!"

Shirley looked at her wide-eyed and with a look of alarm. "No, you're not, dear. Perhaps we should just sit here for a minute and chat. Do you remember what happened?"

Clara concentrated for a few minutes. "Yes. Last night. Lucy. She knocked over the shelf and I fell." Panic was now on her face. "Oh, my God, is Lucy all right?"

Shirley patted her hand in reply. "She's right as rain and not missing a single one of her nine lives, which is more than I can say for you."

Clara looked back at her friend. "But I'm missing a life, Shirley, and I need to find it. I need to find him. I need to find Hamish."

Shirley looked directly back at her and pursed her lips. "The only thing you'll be doing, young lady, is taking a visit to the hospital. Everything else can wait."

∼

Several hours later, the doctor had given her the once over, cleaned her wound, given her three stitches and pronounced her safe to go home. That, however, was not enough for Shirley, who insisted that she should stay overnight with Clara just to be sure. After Shirley had tidied up the mess, Clara sorted through the pieces that could be glued together and set them aside. Her favourite piece was a Royal Dalton ballerina whose one leg had broken just above the knee. She easily fixed it and set it aside with the others while Shirley made some tea.

"Here you go. Would you like a biscuit to go with that?"

"No thanks."

"I know I keep asking but are you sure you're all right, dear? You seemed to be away with the fairies when I found you. You asked if I was Bessie."

Clara took a sip of her tea and shook her head, finding it hard to explain. "Only because you reminded me of her." After a minute of silence, she spoke again. "I think I went somewhere. But not in a dream—a real place where I was someone else in another time."

"Like a past life experience?"

"Yes, but more than that. I was really there. There was a man I loved, and I made him promise to find me again. I think I died, and I don't know what happened to him. I know it sounds odd, but I need to find him. I need to know he's all right."

Shirley sat silent for a while watching Clara. "I think you've had a very powerful reincarnation experience." Hand over her mouth, she leaned back in the chair and closed her eyes deep in thought. "It's got to be the book. I knew it was important, but I didn't know why."

Clara shook her head. "I don't understand." And then it dawned on her. "The book was dedicated to Klara. Do you think he meant me?" Lucy suddenly jumped on her lap and began to knead herself into a comfortable position. Scratching the cat behind her ears, Clara looked back at Shirley. "You know what's odd, before you left the other day you wished me a Scottish New Year's blessing."

"Yes, I'm not sure why."

"I do. Because that's where I went to, Shirley. I went back and found Hamish in Scotland."

"Oh, my, perhaps I should have another look at this book."

"I've put it over there on top of the mantle." As she started to get up, Shirley stopped her.

"No, no, no—you stay put. I'll get it myself."

The moment she touched it Shirley's face changed. Without opening the book, she just held it in her hand and felt the change in the weight, felt the pages rustle with recognition of Clara's presence. She felt the demand for her as strongly as if it were a person in the room with them. The book had power and was drawing Clara into its covers in an attempt to capture her heart. Her face paled as she sat back in her chair and leaned forward towards Clara, who stared back at her with confusion. "This isn't the end of it, Clara, and I'm involved somehow. It seems that I too made a promise. And what's more—he's looking for you too."

A LEAP OF FATE

CHAPTER NINE

Oxford 1860

*P*rofessor Michael H. Chamberlain II, flicked an errant speck of ash off of his spotless suit and carried on walking down St Michael's Street towards the Bodleian Library. Opened in 1602, it was the main research institution in Oxford, and one of the oldest libraries in Europe. He took great pride at having access to it and quickened his steps in anticipation. With any luck, today's interview would change his life. Recent growth within the library meant the expansion into a nearby building known as the Radcliffe Camera. Medical and scientific collections were currently being transferred and new book acquisitions were being acquired from Italy. There was an opening position and he meant it to be his. Fortunately for him, luck would not need to play any part in it. His father, an honoured alma mater had contributed heavily to the library, and as far as he was concerned, the interview would simply be a formality. Still, he was nervous, a sign that he wanted it too much.

The position was one that he was well-suited for, but it would also mean spending the next several months in Italy, away from the pressure of the marital expectations of his family. He kept reminding himself that this was an excellent opportunity and not just a reason to escape Margaret. It's not that he didn't like her, he did, and in all fairness, she seemed to be a very nice person. It was just that they were so different.

Margaret Louise Hudson was the only daughter of Thomas Hudson, owner of Hudson and Clark, a locomotive building company in Yorkshire, England. She had been properly educated in art and decorum, as expected by a wealthy family, but sadly, intellect was not a characteristic that she could justifiably claim. She was in fact, a silly girl whose conversations centred around other silly people and what those silly people did. The problem was that his family could not see past the financial benefit of the merger.

He and Margaret had known each other since childhood and although nothing formal had ever been stated, the weight of the expectation that something eventually *would*, pressed down on his independent spirit. He enjoyed a good laugh as well as anyone else, but he also had a serious side. It was important for him to make something of himself, independent of his family's wealth. He wanted to make his own mark upon the world and Italy beckoned. Margaret Louise Hudson, did not.

Arriving at the Bodleian, he gave his overcoat another quick brush then proceeded to speak to a white-haired older gentleman at the desk. "Good morning, sir. My name is Professor Michael Chamberlain, and I am here to see Professor William Doyle."

"Certainly, sir. I believe he's expecting you. Do you know where you're going?"

"I do indeed." Giving the gentleman a nod of appreciation for his assistance, Professor Chamberlain climbed the dark oaken stairs to the second level and continued down the long hallway. The carved ceilings and stacks of ancient manuscripts infused his spirit and thrilled his senses. Closing his eyes briefly, he took in a deep breath. There was a scent to ancient tomes, exuding a tangible history that only the Bodleian could capture. It called out to him to stop, peruse and linger. He didn't though.

At the end of the corridor, to the right, was a small office with an ancient dark wooden bench parked in the hallway outside the door. The hall was silent and for a moment he wasn't sure whether he should just sit or knock on the door. Opting to knock, he rapped lightly on the door.

From within came a familiar raspy voice with a deep Irish brogue. "Aye. Come in."

As he entered the cramped office, he was immediately struck by the stacks of books towering the walls, chairs, floor and any available nook. Professor Doyle smiled and nodded to the only empty chair to his left.

"Have a seat, Professor Chamberlain."

A wisp of a man, he donned a grey speckled, neatly trimmed beard with a mustache, balding head and pince-nez glasses that were attached to a chain that hung down his cheek. He was neatly attired with a forest green vest, overcoat and tie, overtop a starched white shirt.

As he took off his coat, Michael quickly looked around for somewhere to place it, but seeing nowhere available, simply folded it, and hung it over the arm of the chair. With a quick smile, he sat and waited for Professor Doyle to initiate the conversation. And continued to wait. Finally, after a full minute of silence, that felt like five, he cleared his throat and opened his mouth to speak. But it was the Professor who absent-mindedly broke the silence.

"Well, Professor Chamberlain, I can see no hindrance to you taking this position. Your references are impressive and of course your father's reputation is second to none. We'll expect nothing less from you of course, and we'll need you to book your passage as soon as possible. You'll go to Rome first and then travel on to Florence for a discussion with the Uffizi Gallery. We have a contact there that has given us some excellent references to an estate library that we are anxious to acquire. There's also another gentleman there, a James Brydon, that if time permits, I'd appreciate you meeting with. Not quite in your discipline I'm afraid, but he has some rare books on religious studies. I'd appreciate it greatly if you could have a look at their condition and approximate value."

"Yes, sir, it would be my pleasure."

"Good, we'll book you in some local pensiones, all expenses paid of course. Any questions?"

"No, sir. Thank you, sir."

"Good. Mrs. Martin will be in contact with you in regards to paperwork, contracts, travel matters and inoculations etc. As for me, here's a list of the acquisitions we're interested in. We'll be in touch."

And that was that. Evidently dismissed, he was left with the impression that although he seemed to have secured the position, the interview had never happened.

CHAPTER TEN

*A*fter two months of preparation and travel, Michael stepped down from the British Cunard gangplank on to the Italian shores at Civita Vecchia. He had, of course, previously been to Italy in his younger years when he had done the obligatory, "Grand Tour" with his mates from university; however, the purpose for that trip was far different than his current focus. All young men from wealthy families were expected to take the Grand Tour. Parents felt that the opportunity for them to "sew their wild oats", so to speak, finished them off; with their young men returning more-worldly, more polished, cultured and better prepared to take on family duties. However, the reality for all those young men from wealthy families was several months (or two years as in the case of his friend Baxter) of drinking, intimate relations with the fairer sex and the obligatory excursions to see the sites. His own trip had been no different, and this time he was excited to see Italy as it should be seen, or at least certainly through a less-alcoholic lens.

The last leg of the trip required pooling a carriage into Rome which he shared with another couple and their gangly son of roughly thirteen years. The woman, in her late thirties, was tall and all sharp angles in contrast to her shorter, rotund husband. Her pinched cheeks and pursed lips dominated her face and was likely a strong indication of her personality. Polite nods were acknowledged with the usual introductions and pleasantries exchanged, and it wasn't long before the woman began to take in her surroundings with an obvious distaste. Running a finger across the dusty window she tut-tutted her disgust. "Thank heavens I had the foresight to wear my second-best travelling gloves, Mr. Foster. Why, just look at this filth." Her husband, obviously used to her sensitivities, gave a quick look towards Michael, then wordlessly tipped his hat lower to cover his eyes.

Ignoring his indifference, she looked outside towards the offending carriage owner and declared her judgement. "Mark my words, I'll be writing this in my journals for my Ladies group to read."

There was no question as to who ruled the roost in this family.

Suddenly realizing her tired son was leaning against the carriage, she rebuked him sharply. "John! Sit up properly this instance! If I've told you once, I've told you a thousand times, a proper gentleman does not slouch." She turned to Michael for support. "Wouldn't you agree Mr.... I'm so sorry, I've forgotten your name."

Michael gave a quick nod. "Chamberlain, Madame. Professor Michael H. Chamberlain II."

Her eyes lit up as he introduced himself. "Ah, yes. Professor Chamberlain."

Obviously, the opportunity to continue haranguing her son was too great for the woman to pass up.

"See here before you, John, a Professor and a gentleman. I assure you he did not get where he is today by being a slouch."

Michael felt the youth's pain and looked towards his dark eyes with a tinge of a smile. "I can assure you, young man, that my own mother complained of the same thing when I was your age. You may feel hard-put now, but what she says has merit."

As the young man unhappily straightened his posture,

Michael took out a small book from his carpet bag and with a smile and a nod to Mrs. Foster, began to read.

An hour later, after the cabbie dropped off the Fosters at the train station, they drove down Via Del Corso and arrived at the Grand Hotel Plaza in central Rome. It was a magnificent building, having been recently renovated from what had previously been the home of Piemonte nobility. Struck by the lavish and ornate splendor of the building, Michael congratulated himself on his good fortune. He would likely be here for a month or two, before moving on to Florence for several more months after that.

After being shown to his room, there was enough time before dinner to wander through some of the grander chambers. The Great Salon was a magnificent room of ornate windows and gilded ceilings that surpassed some of the most magnificent palaces. Through the front windows he could glimpse the street, but as much as he wanted to go outside, he hesitated. He needed to eat and seeing how tomorrow he would begin his new position, he needed a good night's sleep. But the street beckoned, and for some reason he couldn't help but follow.

All of his senses were assaulted at once. Peasant-carts, some laden with wine-barrels, others with wood faggots, jingled by to the din of horses' hooves on cobblestones. Noisy shouts from vendors, boys yelling at each other as they ran through the streets, music from an upstairs window and everywhere, delivery men carrying baskets of various vegetables over their shoulders. Despite being tired from travelling, Michael began to feel energized. He decided he wouldn't go far and reasoned that a bit of fresh air would help him sleep. Looking both ways he was unsure of which way to turn, until a small group of young men walked past laughing. Rapidly bantering back and forth in Italian he caught the occasional word, *vino* and *la donna*. Chuckling to himself, he concluded that some things never change.

Following the flow of pedestrians, he slowed his pace and ambled along, occasionally stopping to look into shop windows or admire a building's architecture.

The city was alive with passion and bit by bit the weight of his family's expectations fell away. He was his own man here. He had money and an excellent position. There was a sense of excitement here from the depth of his soul that he hadn't felt in a long while. Was it any wonder why the British enjoyed Italy so much? But it was more than that. He pondered how the study of classics was considered an essential part of any upper-class education in England. Why in his own youth, up to three-quarters of his studies was spent on Greek and Latin. Consequently, he associated Italy with that which he had studied, and therefore, projected his love and high esteem for the ancient civilization onto the Italy he saw before him. The cobblestones upon where his footsteps tread for instance, were enchanted with thousands of memories that rose up and chased each other. The air was charmed, and he was too spellbound by the past to think only of the present.

Lost in his lofty thoughts, he stopped abruptly to look up at a unique piece of architecture, thereby causing someone to bump into him from behind. This mishap resulted in an immediate torrent of Italian fury from what appeared to be a young woman.

Her Italian was fired off so fast and so furious, that the only word he caught was *stupida*. He turned to apologise. But as he did so, a book she was carrying fell to the ground and as they both stooped to get it, they bumped heads, or more correctly, bumped hats. The frustrated woman lowered her head in order to secure her wide-brimmed hat with one hand and attempted to grab the book with the other. However, Michael's arms were longer and in that precise moment, when he handed it back to her and first looked upon her face, fate played her wily hand. Cool blue eyes and wild auburn hair captured his attention immediately and so forcefully and deeply that she took his breath away. He stumbled out his apology like a freshman.

"Mi scusi, Signora. I apologize. I am so sorry."

Dressed in a white linen gown that accentuated her slim figure, she appeared to be in her mid-twenties. Her face was classically beautiful with a Cupid's bow mouth that slowly curled into a reluctant smile. In perfect English she replied, "I should have known—another Englishman entranced by Rome."

He nodded enthusiastically. "Yes, absolutely. Guilty as charged." As he smiled back and played with the rim of his hat, he was really noting what an exquisitely beautiful creature she was and desperately began to think of something clever to say. "My name is Michael Chamberlain, Professor Chamberlain, actually, and if I've ruined your book, I would be more than happy to replace it for you."

She smiled again and looked up at him with soft eyes. *Was it just him or did she feel the connection as well?* "Thank you, Professor Chamberlain, that's most kind of you, but I really must be going. You see, I am meeting with my friend and I am already late."

As she began to walk away, he groaned inside at his ineptitude with women, desperate to say anything to see her again, he blurted out. "Perhaps we could meet again."

Turning around, she playfully walked backwards for a few steps then grinned, raised her chin and cheekily replied, "Perhaps!"

Michael's heart raced—was that a yes? He walked towards her not wanting to be pushy but also not wanting to lose her. "When?"

"When we meet again, Professor Chamberlain, or don't you believe in fate?"

"Your name? Can you tell me your name?"

But she was gone, leaving him standing in the street staring at two old women dressed in black chatting away, a vendor selling roasted chestnuts and a group of ladies consulting their Baedeker.

As he slowly walked back to the hotel he felt as if, in some strange grand scheme of the universe, the sole purpose of his walk was to bump into her. Something had shifted in his world and he knew with a certainty that he couldn't explain, that they would see each other again. And what was more important—so did she.

~

The next month flew by in a blur of meetings, introductions and acquisitions. Escorted around by his translator and guide Paulo, Michael had very little time to enjoy the city or the food. With so many British ex-pats and tourists, the hotel served typical British fare to accommodate his countrymen's lack of culinary adventure. When he had some time, Michael promised himself that he would enjoy some traditional Italian cuisine. However, what was constantly in the back of his mind was the young woman with the book.

His assistant, Paulo Rossi, was a young man with an infectious sense of humour that had pulled Michael, more than once, out of a dark mood. Paulo was at least ten years younger than Michael, and he seemed to know everyone and was acknowledged by all with a friendly smile. When Michael asked him how it was possible for him to remember so many names, he laughed and said it was easy as he was related to most of them. He had quit school at the age of ten, as he had to help provide for his mother and brother and sisters. He was a quick learner and had a curious mind, and Michael enjoyed his company very much.

One afternoon, after Michael had successfully secured several scientific manuscripts from an estate sale, he found himself without anything to do. "Paulo, are you up for an adventure? I would love to taste authentic Italian cooking and am at a loss as to where to go or what to eat. What say you if you join me and be my food guide for the evening?"

"Absolutely Professor, but if you really want to taste authentic Italian, we have to go and visit my Nona. She's the best cook I know, even better than my mother, but don't ever tell her that."

"That would be wonderful, Paulo, but perhaps we should warn her first of company."

Paulo shook his head and waved his hand. "No, no, no professor, my family was already going there for dinner, one more won't be a problem."

"Are you sure?"

"I'm telling you, professor, she would be insulted if I didn't bring you. I'm warning you though, she's a seer."

"A seer?"

"Si, like a *zingaro*, a gypsy, a teller of fortunes. Sometimes she sees things, so don't take any notice if she does."

"Thank you, Paulo. It sounds like a very adventurous evening ahead."

CHAPTER ELEVEN

*P*aulo's Nona lived in a tiny village several miles outside of Rome, and as the carriage took them down narrow streets beyond the hotel district, the height of the houses made the narrow streets gloomy, even at midday. The houses, although large, took on a look of dereliction, as if they had been left empty for years and were now occupied by tenants who were too poor to keep them from falling into decay. Everywhere, there were holes in the walls where the scaffolding had been fixed. From the windowsills and from ropes fastened across the streets, half-washed rags and clothing of every variety fluttered in the breeze.

As they left the city gates, a pack-horse nibbled blades of grass between the stones, while a sentinel on duty stared listlessly as their carriage passed by. A beggar, squatting by the roadside, cried out for charity, "*Per l'amore di Dio e della Santa Vergine*", while a troop of priests passed by on the other side. A hillock-covered plain of half common, half pastureland, surrounded the city where, every now and then, a drove of wild, shaggy buffaloes grazed lazily. At first, it appeared almost desolate. The landscape was dotted with a few stunted trees, a deserted house or two, and here and there, a crumbling mass of shapeless brickwork. There was hardly any traffic, apart from a few rough carts loaded with charcoal, and a string of mules who were almost buried beneath high piles of brushwood which were slung in panniers across their backs.

As they drove on, the uncultivated mountain slopes gradually became lush and green. The rolling hills, scented with wild thyme and mountain oregano, stirred Michael's senses as the afternoon sun warmed his cheeks. He felt at peace, and as the clop, clop from the horse's hooves provided its own natural rhythm, he allowed his thoughts to drift to the young woman. Was he being silly? Would he ever see her again? In two weeks time he would be in Florence, and by then he would have missed his chance. He remembered every moment of their meeting and savoured her smile, those eyes and that hair. It was as if they had already known each other before. Was she looking for him? Would he see her again before he left Rome?

As the horse and buggy rounded the corner, the house came into view, offering up a picturesque watercolour of rural Italian life.

Paulo's Nona's white-washed villa was nestled at the top of a gentle slope that was dotted with a grove of olive trees growing on the left, while lemon trees, heavy with fruit, surrounded the property to the front and to the right. If he had any artistic abilities at all, Michael would have painted this scene immediately. As they got closer, the ancient villa revealed her delicacy, where unused cornices lay in the mud, while the doors and large blotches on her façade indicated where the plaster had peeled away.

He smiled at the large rustic table near the shade of a tree that was fitted with old chairs of every size and style. An older woman, that Paolo pointed out was his mother, appeared to be wiping it down. Over to the side where a little girl was twirling herself around and around, was another smaller table filled with pots of herbs and red geraniums.

His mother, upon hearing the carriage, looked over, smiling, and then noting a visitor, began to walk towards them. As soon as they had descended from the carriage, their arrival was met by several children of various ages, from a toddler to a child of around ten, who were all smiling, clamoring for Paulo's attention and eyeing his visitor with interest.

From inside the villa, an old woman with white hair pinned back into a bun stepped out into the sunshine, holding on to her cane for support, followed by a man and woman. As Michael was greeted warmly with smiles and the traditional double kiss, they didn't speak any English, but their sentiments were clear: he was welcome.

Paulo made the introductions and Michael did his best to speak in Italian, which, in many cases, caused howls of laughter from the children. His aunt and uncle spoke a little English, so with the help of Paulo, the conversation was enjoyable, with most of their questions being about England. The children endlessly asked him how to say words like goodnight, or hello, or dog, and then hilariously practised saying them with an English accent.

Wine was poured and continued to flow throughout the evening, and he honestly couldn't remember having a finer time. The food was as excellent as Paulo had said it would be. It was simple fare, pasta and a sauce, freshly baked bread, tomatoes off the vine with fragrant basil and farmer's cheese, but everything was so fresh, it was fit for a king.

Michael caught the eye of a little girl who was around five years old, she shyly looked away, but this made him idly wonder whether he would ever have children of his own.

As the sun began to set, Michael rose with the others to help bring in the dishes, but Nona, who had been staring at him with a funny look on her face, took his hand and asked Paulo to follow. Michael gave Paulo a look, who merely shrugged as if to say, I warned you.

Speaking in Italian to her grandson, Nona suddenly stopped and waited for Paulo to explain to Michael.

"Nona says to sit. She says she has a message for you."

While Nona made herself comfortable in an over-stuffed chair, she instructed Michael (by using her hands) to sit in a wooden chair, close enough to her so she could take his hand. Michael, having drank his fair share of wine, was happy to comply. She then indicated for Paulo to sit nearby so he could translate.

"Si, si," he nodded, and pulled up another wooden chair as both men sat in silence waiting for Nona to begin.

The old woman closed her eyes, and from her apron pocket pulled out a rosary and began to mumble. Paulo looked towards Michael and gave him a quick smile. Putting his palms together he indicated that she was praying.

Suddenly her eyes opened wide, and she seemed to stare at Michael, only he didn't have the sense that it was him that she was seeing. After a few minutes of uncomfortable silence, she spoke to Paulo in rapid Italian. In turn he repeated her words. "She says to tell you that there is a woman that you loved once in another lifetime and you have been searching for her ever since."

Nona held his hands tighter, her eyebrows crossed, as if straining to see something clearer.

"She says that you both made a promise to find each other again."

Nona said a few more words.

"There are two women and two choices. The easy choice will make you very unhappy and end badly. Better she says to be a bachelor than marry."

Paulo then asked his Nona about the second choice, and she replied with a look of sadness in her voice.

Paulo nodded and turned back to Michael. "She says there is great sacrifice in the second choice, one that you may not be ready to make. Better to wait until you meet again."

She spoke again at length until Paulo held up his hand for her to stop.

"Okay, okay. Nona." Turning to Michael he explained. "She says, Michael, that there is no question that you two are meant to be together. She is your soulmate and the only woman you will ever love. The only woman you were meant to be with. But to love is to also allow her to fly with her own wings. This woman is very independent, but currently in a situation not of her control. She needs to be strong for her own self before she can take your hand. You must allow her to do this, or the consequences will last further into the future than you realize. She says you're a good man and this woman is worth waiting for."

Michael was speechless and confused. The best he could do was mutter a *grazie* and lean in to give her a hug. Whether her reading was accurate or not, he was touched by the intent and consideration behind it. Yet she had picked up on two women. One a certain mistake—Margaret, and the other, not right now. *The woman with the book?*

A week later Michael received word that he was required to travel to Florence earlier than expected. Apparently, an estate sale had come up and the University was eager to acquire the entire library. He was to review the library for himself as well as meet with James Brydon—the gentleman that Professor Doyle had recommended. With a heavy heart, he left Rome and boarded the train for Florence, all the while thinking about the girl with the book.

CHAPTER TWELVE

*M*ichael arrived at the *Stazione di Maria Antonia*, so named, according to his Baedeker, in honour of Princess Maria Antonia of the two Sicillies. This was his first trip to Florence, and he was looking forward to exploring it completely.

As he stood opposite the Santa Maria Novella church, he gazed up at the façade in appreciation, referring once more to his travel guide. He read that it was designed in the Italian Gothic-style, with the construction being completed in 1350, while the marble facade had been completed by Alberti in the Renaissance style over a hundred years later.

However, Michael was here for the libraries. The *Riccardiana* and *Moreniana* libraries adjoining the Medici Palace had the most complete collection, including valuable manuscripts, of works on Tuscan history. The *Gabinetto Scientifico e Letterario* was a scientific and literary library founded in 1819 by Jean-Baptiste Vieusseux, the central figure of a group that included the leading literary figures of Italy at that time.

While he was in Rome, Michael had already been warned that the Florentines were exactly as Dante had characterized them; tight-fisted, envious and haughty. He had read that after Lorenzo de' Medici transferred the University of Florence to Pisa in 1473, the medical school remained behind, leading the scientific movement in Italy. Rome may have been beautiful, but Florence had his heart. And why wouldn't it? Looking around, he agreed with that notion: Florence was a jewel.

Hiring a small hackney cab, his initial plan was to settle himself into the pensione the University had arranged and then meet up with Mr. Brydon to discuss arrangements to see his collection. With a sense of excitement, the driver pulled up at the pensione and waited as Michael stepped inside to confirm his lodging arrangements. However, his excitement was short lived. Due to the sudden change in plans, the University had forgotten to contact the Signora about his earlier arrival, so his room would not be free until the following week.

Frustrated, he checked the time and realized that he would not have enough time to find another room-to-let and still make his meeting with James Brydon. He was left with no other choice but to leave his luggage with the Signora and collect it later. This was going to be a very long day indeed.

Directing the cabbie to the address he was given, the driver took Michael south of the Arno, where an elegant villa stood gracefully at the end of a long driveway, that was lined with Cyprus trees and various marble statues. He was both immediately impressed at the obvious wealth, and curious as to the size and scope of the library in question.

He knocked on the door and was greeted by a tall, slim, middle-aged butler who appeared to be expecting his arrival. Then, after the usual process of taking Michael's hat and coat and announcing him, he was immediately escorted through a magnificent hallway into a study. An older gentleman who looked well into his late-seventies, gingerly rose from his chair and fumbled for his cane that lay against his desk. Dressed in a smart Italian silk smoking jacket and a silk necktie, his white hair seemed to make up its own mind in terms of direction, and his bushy white mustache all but covered his friendly smile.

"Ah, Professor Chamberlain, I am James Brydon. I am so pleased you were able to make it. Please have a seat," said James Brydon, as they shook hands.

As fragile as James Brydon's physical self seemed to be, his voice was strong, with a delightful touch of an Italian accent. He gestured to two red-velvet padded chairs situated by a large leaded window. A small table sat between them. The older man then turned to his Butler. "Antonio, perhaps you could bring some wine for our guest, or would you prefer tea, Professor Chamberlain?"

"Actually, a cup of tea would be quite appreciated right now, thank you."

Antonio nodded a "very good, sir", and then looked to his employer. "Oh, yes, tea will be fine for me as well, Antonio."

As his butler left the room, James looked back at his guest. "I trust your travel here wasn't too tiresome."

"No, not at all."

"And your lodgings are suitable?"

"Well, to be honest, sir, that's a bit of a muddle right now. I'm afraid my earlier arrival wasn't conveyed in time to the Signora, so I'll be searching for something suitable until my original booking can be honoured next week. It's a bit of a pickle, but I'm sure I'll be able to sort it all out later."

Mr. Brydon gave him a hard look, knitting his brows as he did so. "Well, we can't have that. You'll stay here and I'll hear no more about it." Picking up his bell, he bellowed again for his butler. "Antonio!"

Michael was embarrassed at his predicament. "That's quite generous of you, sir, but I hate to impose."

"Nonsense, Professor Chamberlain. I've a very large house with only myself and my niece to fill it up. You'd be a very welcome guest, and of course free to come and go as it pleases you. We don't stand on pomp and decorum here."

Arriving a moment later, Antonio awaited his orders.

"Antonio, please tell Signora Ponari to have the guest room

made up. Professor Chamberlain will be staying with us for at least a week."

Turning to Michael he queried. "And your luggage?"

"I'm afraid I left it in the care of the pensione until later."

"Not a problem. Antonio will arrange for it to be brought here, won't you Antonio?"

Antonio nodded and smiled at his employer. "Of course, sir. It will be done immediately."

Michael leaned forward to express his gratitude. "Thank you again, sir. This is very kind of you."

"Not at all, Michael, is it? I'll let you in on a little secret. It's been just myself and my niece for so long that I'll appreciate some male conversation. She's a lovely girl my Klara, but these modern girls with their independent ways... Tell you what, after our tea, why don't you relax and freshen up. I usually have a nap around this time, but Antonio can help you with whatever you need. You'll have plenty of time to see the library now that you'll be staying here."

"I'd appreciate that. It's been a long day."

"Klara won't be home until later. She'll join us for dinner of course. Lovely girl, although, to be honest, a bit too much like her Florentine mother. Caterina was quite the beauty in her day. Klara certainly takes after her mother in that respect. Dear me, my brother didn't stand a chance. God rest their souls. Tragically they died in a fire when Klara was only six."

"I'm very sorry to hear that."

"Far too young to be orphaned, but there you have it. She's been with me ever since. Although I'm hardly a replacement for a mother and father. You see I've never had children of my own, but I've done my best, spoiled her rotten and love her dearly."

～

After his rest, Michael felt quite refreshed. His luggage had been delivered and what could have been a challenging day was turning out quite well. His only quandary at this point was how to dress for dinner. Assuming he would have been pre-warned if it were formal, he dressed as any gentleman should, in a plain white shirt with small pleats and a black waistcoat and black tie and paid particular attention to his hair and outward appearance. He smiled as his father's words resounded in his head: "A gentleman makes himself admired for his wit, not his *toilette*; his elegance and refinement, not the price of his clothes." Only then, when he was satisfied with every last detail, did he proceed to make his way down the stairs to the dining room where fate was about to play her second hand.

CHAPTER THIRTEEN

*S*itting in a chair at the base of the stairs was his host, who was impeccably dressed in a black suit and tie. He smiled as Michael descended the stairs and used his cane to steady himself as he stood up. "I thought we'd have a drink first, Michael. Klara should be here soon. You don't mind me calling you Michael, do you?"

"Not at all, sir, and how would you prefer me to address you?"

"Well Klara calls me Tups, but my given name is James, so I suppose you can call me that."

"It would be my pleasure, James."

Directing him into an elegant study of dark wood and leather panelled walls, James poured them both a brandy, and after a brief toast to friendship, Michael took a sip. But just as he was about to tell James how much he admired his taste in Brandy, a woman's voice rang through the halls.

"Tups? Tups, I'm back and I'm famished. Where are you, so I can give you a hug before I get dressed for dinner? I've had such a day!"

James smiled indulgently and nodded to Michael. "Prepare yourself for Hurricane Klara." In the next moment a tumble of auburn hair and blue silk came swishing through the door and a familiar slender figure embraced her uncle. *It was her.*

She quickly turned noticing that a guest was also in the room and with a spark of recognition looked deeply into his eyes. She smiled. "It's you."

He in turn fumbled out, "You're not in Rome." Then immediately wanted to kick himself for stating the obvious. *How could this be?*

She giggled her response. "No, I'm not, but I was." She then turned to her uncle, who looked quite confused. "Tups, this gentleman and I quite literally bumped into each other in Rome, on the street. Or rather I bumped into him."

Michael was quick to jump in this time. "Yes, but had I not stopped so suddenly, I wouldn't have caused you to drop your book. It was entirely my fault. I trust it's no worse for wear?"

"Absolutely fine, I assure you." She knitted her brows. "But how do you come to be here?"

Her uncle quickly interrupted. "My dear, how about you get yourself changed for dinner where we can discuss this further. Now off you go and don't be too long. Cook will have our head if her dinner is spoiled due to your tardiness."

At the mention of the cook, she widened her eyes in faux fear, then kissing her uncle quickly on the cheek, she gave Michael a quick smile and hurried out.

Michael could barely contain his joy at seeing her again. In fact, he couldn't ever remember being so famished. Any attempt at small talk with James seemed to be lost in a cloud.

At long last she descended the stairs causing him to catch his breath. Dressed in green satin, her dress was ornamented by bouillons en tablier and black lace up the centre. The high waist-line and tight sleeves showed off her slim figure, while her thick auburn hair was styled in long curls and a green velvet ribbon. He was speechless.

"My dear niece, how lovely you look tonight."

"Thank you, uncle." Slowly raising her eyes to Michael, she blushed as he nodded his appreciation.

"I must agree."

What followed was an awkward silence.

Her uncle gave a little cough. "Well, I suppose I should introduce you two before one of you explodes. Klara, this is Professor Michael H. Chamberlain II from the Bodleian Library in Oxford. He's here to discuss my library of religious studies. Professor Chamberlain, Michael, may I present my niece, Miss Klara Elizabeth Brydon. And now that we have the formalities over with, shall we dine?"

Klara entered the dining hall with her uncle at her side as Michael followed close behind.

Antonio, who was properly attired in formal livery, pulled out her chair, and the men took their places. As they were a small group, James sat at the head, and Klara and Michael faced each other on each side. The table was elegantly set with silver and china. Michael looked across at Klara and smiled. The candlelight caught her beauty in a way that made his pulse race. There was something so familiar about her. Was it the way she turned her head when thinking about an answer, or her eyes, or even her laughter; he couldn't say. Only that there was something about her that made him feel as if he had known her forever.

Her voice brought him back to the present. "Have you seen much of Florence as yet, Professor Chamberlain?"

"No, not at all. Perhaps you would be so kind as to recommend the best sites Miss Brydon?"

"I could, but I suppose that depends on whether you are interested in seeing our city through the eyes of a tourist or a traveller?"

"I'm not sure that I understand. Are they not the same?"

She laughed. "Not at all. The traveller is in search of people and adventure. They immerse themselves in the experience. While tourists are a passive lot, expecting interesting things to come their way, everything to be done for them. They want a pleasant experience without the inconvenience of travel. Tourists see our country through a window but not at the table where they could taste our food. So, Professor, are you a traveller or a tourist?"

Michael smiled, looked down at his food and shook his head. "You're very eloquent, Miss Brydon, and were I to have been a tourist I would certainly be immediately converted to a traveller."

James raised his glass. "Well stated, sir. Now Klara, give the man some peace. Michael, what is your discipline in your studies?"

"History, sir, but I have a personal interest in the religious studies of various cultures."

"Really, how interesting. I may have a book you might be interested in. It's on metempsychosis. Quite a fascinating read actually."

"Are you familiar with this belief, Professor?" asked Klara.

"Yes, at least a little. Academically, the theory of metempsychosis, or reincarnation, states that energy never dies. It's transferred back and forth endlessly, occupying different dwellings or bodies. Once energy escapes an expired body, it's only a matter of time until it re-enters a new one."

Klara tilted her head. "I'm curious, Professor..."

He interrupted and spoke softly. "Please call me Michael."

"Very well... Michael. My uncle says that if someone dies leaving unfinished business, their spirit will reincarnate into circles where they not only felt most loved, but also into situations that allow them to resolve what was left unfinished. Do you believe this?"

He blushed deeply. "I do, yes."

"And do you believe that lovers reincarnate?"

For some unexplainable reason his heart pounded. "I do. Well, at least I'd like to. And what about you, Miss Klara?"

"I lean towards the sciences myself..." she lowered her head and slowly looked back at him, "at least I did."

James finished his soup and sat back seemingly oblivious to

what had just transpired. "There was a situation in India I believe, where a three-year-old child remembered the exact details of her past life, including her name, where she lived and her husband's name. The account was documented by an old colleague of mine and he has assured me that every detail was true."

"That's quite remarkable, especially to remember a name."

Klara dabbed her mouth with a napkin and smiled. "What does the 'H' stand for in your name?"

"Hamish—it's an old family name from Scotland."

Klara blushed and attempted an air of amusement. "Ah, my favourite name, Professor Chamberlain." But when she looked back at Michael, she knew he had caught the slightest of recognition in her eyes. Recovering from her self-conscious blush, she held her wine glass up as if in a toast. Something was stirring in her soul. "To old family names."

CHAPTER FOURTEEN

*T*he following morning, Michael rose early in the hopes of sharing breakfast with Klara but was met only by James reading his morning paper.

"Ah Professor, you're up. Excellent. I trust you slept well?"

"I did indeed, sir."

"And you've been well-attended to?"

"I have. Your staff have been more than helpful."

"Good. Good. I thought we'd spend our morning in the library, and I do so want to show you that book. Klara is off at her studies and won't be back till later."

"Her studies?"

"Oh, yes. I'm surprised she didn't bring it up herself over dinner last night. My niece is a very clever girl, although she's dug quite a difficult path for herself. I warned her of course, as is my duty, but she is ever so headstrong. It was easier to let her have her way. Whatever comes of it though, she'll handle it."

Michael must have looked confused because the old man chuckled and then carried on.

"Medicine. She has set her sights to be a medical physician for women. She would certainly be the very first one, at least in Italy."

"In England as well, I believe. That's quite the goal. And has she been accepted, by the profession, or in particular by men?"

"Not at all. But they don't know Klara. Her marks are excellent, and her mind is sharp. There's no issue of her not being up to the task. She'll continue to study until they give in. Even if it takes her thirty years."

"And surely she must have a suitor. What does he think?"

"Phh, my dear boy, I've given up on that account. An intellectual woman does not seem to be what most men want these days. Besides, she'll inherit whatever I have. She'll not be left wanting on that account."

"She appears to be an amazing young woman."

"She is indeed. Now let's have a look at my library, shall we? Frankly, I'm ready for my pipe and I'm anxious for you to see my collection."

~

Later that afternoon, Klara returned early, her cheeks flushed from the cooler weather outside. As she popped her head into the library, she was greeted by the heartwarming sight of her uncle contentedly reading, pipe in hand, while Michael sat comfortably in an over-stuffed chair in the corner. It struck her that this was a scene that she could grow used to. Michael was someone she could grow used to. Stepping further into the room, she boldly suggested that she show Michael some sites. James looked up from his book and raised an eyebrow as if to speak, but wisely put his head back down and carried on as if he had not heard a thing.

A short time later, dressed warmly against the cooler elements, Michael offered his arm to Klara and the two stepped out. "Have you any preference, Michael, or will you trust me as your guide."

He grinned. "I am in your capable hands, m'lady."

"Well, that's something I don't hear very often."

He stopped and looked directly at her. "Perhaps you should."

Rewarded with the hint of a crooked smile, he patted her hand and nodded towards the street. "Shall we?"

They took a carriage to an L-shaped square in front of the Palazzo Vecchio which was filled with every sort of person, from tourists, to soldier, to locals. There Michael watched Florentines, from those who were wealthy to peasants, gathered in various settings. Some sat in contemplation while others sat in quiet repose. Some chatted with friends while others stood as still as the statues they were marvelling at. For the second time in his life, Michael sorely wished that he could paint.

Clara's soft voice broke the spell. "This is Piazza della Signoria, the main point of history for the Florentine Republic. It has been the scene of important events of the city since 1115, when the Florentines rebelled against the Margraviate of Tuscany." She then pointed towards a granite slab in the pavement towards the centre of the piazza. "The Dominican brother Girolamo Savonarola, was hanged and burned right there in 1498. In fact, it is said that almost all of the history of Florence has passed in this square. At the ringing of the bell over Palazzo Vecchio, the Florentines would gather to approve new laws or to defend city institutions. Feasts, shows and tournaments have all been organized here."

"Fascinating. And I believe this building, with projecting parapets and the tower, is the Palazzo Vecchio. Am I correct?"

Klara smiled at him thoughtfully. "Professor Chamberlain, have you been studying your Baedeker?"

With his crooked grin, he looked for all the world like a guilty schoolboy. "Guilty as charged I'm afraid."

"And shall I quiz you later to make sure you've remembered it all?" she teased.

He looked around and then back at her. "I very much doubt I will forget anything about Florence, including present company I might add."

Perhaps it was the way he looked at her, but something fluttered and stirred inside her soul, like a warm memory of a dream that she couldn't remember, but it felt real, nonetheless. She blushed and stumbled on with an attempt to sound scholastic.

"Beyond the Palazzo Vecchio, between the Piazza and the Arno, stands the Palazzo degli Uffizi. It contains the Archives, the Biblioteca Nazionale, which includes the Palatine and Magliabecchian Libraries and, above all, the great picture gallery that is undoubtedly the finest collection of pictures in the world."

"Ah perfect. I'll be going there tomorrow to meet with someone regarding some acquisitions."

"Well, then, you'll have no trouble finding it." She then took his arm in hers. "Come, let me show you Loggia dei Lanzi."

Overlooking the square towards the corner, was a building consisting of wide arches open to the street where a gallery of statues stood in pride of place.

"It's beautiful."

"Beautiful, yes, but hard won. We Florentines are a difficult and determined lot. That one over there is Perseus, the Greek hero holding up Medusa's severed head by Benvenuto Cellini. They say Cellini burned everything in his household just to make sure the fire was hot enough for the bronze to flow."

"This place is absolutely amazing. I can't imagine that you'd want to live anywhere else."

"People always say that, but for us who see it every day, you forget how special it is. It's nice every now and then to see it through the eyes of a tourist."

"Is there somewhere that you've never been or would like to play tourist?"

"There is actually, and I have no idea why. But I've always wanted to see Scotland."

"Scotland? Really?"

"Yes, I can't explain it, only that it has a magical hold on me. I guess that's why I was a little startled when you said that your middle name was Hamish. A curious coincidence. Have you been?"

"I have. In fact, my family owns some property there. Perhaps one day you'll come and visit so I can repay your uncle's kindness."

"Perhaps I will. How long do you plan on staying, Professor?"

"Please, call me Michael. I insist. I should be here for several more weeks, which will take me into mid-December. I had originally planned to be back home for Christmas. I'm sure my family will be anxious to have me back."

"I imagine they would. If your plans change, you of course would be welcome to share the holidays with us. I think our traditions may be different from what you're used to, but I think you would enjoy them."

"That's most generous of you, but are your celebrations so very different from England?"

Klara held her hand to her cheek and giggled. "Oh, my heavens, yes! In Italy the official beginning of the holiday season is the 8th December and is all about family and food. Christmas Eve, is called *la Vigilia* and traditionally served with no meat. We have a saying in Florence, '*Chi guasta la vigilia di Natale, corpo di lupo e anima di cane*', which issues a curse on those who 'mess up' this meal. Then we attend the Christmas Eve Mass in the Duomo. We have more big dinners on Christmas Day as well as the 26th. Then there's a reprieve of four days before everyone is back at the table for the *Cenone di Capo d'Anno*—the 'big dinner.' This, is followed by lunch on New Year's Day."

"That sounds like a culinary delight in my books."

"Oh, that's not the end. Five days later is the last event of the season, the Epiphany and the arrival of the Three Wise Men and Befana, an ugly old witch who delivers holiday gifts to the children. Finally, on 6th January there is '*l'Epifania tutte le feste si porta via!*', which declares that the holidays are officially over."

Michael smiled. "It sounds lovely. In England, people send pretty Christmas cards to each other. Our family gathers for a large Christmas goose and we have a decorated tree for my nephews, with presents from Father Christmas. Then in the evening, until the wee hours, we tell ghost stories. New Years' Eve all the wealthy families hold open houses, inviting all the local eligible bachelors into their homes to meet their unmarried daughters."

"And do you attend these."

"Unfortunately, for me, it's expected. However, I'll let you in on a little secret… My friends and I go for the libations. Oh, and every year my family hosts a Phantom ball."

"A Phantom ball?"

"Yes, it's a dance or party where guests are expected to dress in ghostly costumes. There's music and card games and because of our Scottish heritage, we celebrate Hogmanay."

"Hogmanay?"

"Hogmanay or 'First Footing' literally means the first foot to cross your threshold after midnight. That person is expected to bring a gift of bread, salt, coal, whisky, food or greenery to ensure a prosperous and healthy year ahead. Then at midnight we all gather in a circle and sing Auld Lang Syne by Robert Burns and link arms for the final stanza."

"That sounds lovely. Do you have a large family Michael?"

"No not at all. I have a younger sister by two years who is married with twin boys, but I have managed to remain a bachelor thus far."

"Not without merit at times, wouldn't you agree?"

"I do indeed. Your uncle told me of your plans to be a physician. I cannot express how impressed I am at your fortitude."

"Thank you, Michael. I cannot say it has been easy, but I am determined to complete my studies. I have never understood why my sex should prohibit me from achieving a goal of which I am passionate and more than capable of. And why shouldn't a woman be a physician to other women? It only makes sense. Bloody men!"

Michael smiled.

"Present company excluded of course. I must admit you seem like a very forward-thinking gentleman. I'm afraid, I don't encounter men such as you very often."

"I'm happy to hear that Klara." He smiled. "I would hate to

think the competition was stiff. I've never been very good at speaking to the opposite sex, moreover, those with little interest outside of gossip and silk. Present company excluded of course."

"Of course. You know Professor, I have been thinking all night about our discussion at dinner on reincarnation and I have the strongest feeling that we knew each other before. Do you think that could be true?"

"I do, Klara." He looked towards the sky, as if the answer was just above. "Perhaps in Scotland?"

She grinned. "Yes, Scotland would do nicely. We're friends aren't we, Michael?"

"I believe we are, Klara. Good friends."

Suddenly her smile brightened. "Are you up for a walk? I think we have just enough time to see my favourite view of the Santa Maria del Fiore Basilica from the Boboli Gardens and still be on time for tea."

"I am in your very capable hands."

They strolled through the streets of Florence, quite content to say nothing. Mostly because so much had already been said, if not implied. Now and then, Klara would point out a statue or something of architectural interest but for the most part she walked with Michael, aware that he was absorbing everything and she, for her part, was comfortable allowing him to do so, without guiding him in a whirlwind of sights.

They stopped at a small shop selling little touristy figurines and fans, to which Klara recommended two items for his mother and sister, and as he casually looked around the store for his nephews, he was touched as he watched her gently pick up a small figurine of a mother and child. He nodded to the merchant to include the little china figure, to which she blushed and said thank you.

They continued to stroll together naturally, comfortably, as if they had all the time in the world. As if they were not counting the minutes they were together. And it was because of this quiet comradery he noticed the lone peasant in a ragged, ill-fitted coat and flat cap sweeping refuse off the dark stone slabs that paved the Florentine streets. As well as the weary woman walking through the streets, with one child in her arm and the other, only a few years older, grasping on to her skirt. The young woman who was hurrying home with an empty basket under her arm. The movers who were lifting a heavy cloth-wrapped piece of furniture, and the grizzled old man with a pipe, quietly watching their efforts. He saw everyday Florence rather than just the highlights —like a traveller and not a tourist.

Klara's voice pulled him out of his gaze. "We'll take the entrance to Boboli through the Pitti Palace."

Just behind the main entrance they crossed the inner courtyard where it opened up to a spectacular garden of centuries-old oak trees, sculptures and fountains.

Her voice was soft and quiet. "This may not be the best day or season to show off the Boboli, but it's my favourite place to walk and I want to share it with you."

She then directed him to a staircase that led up to a large octagonal basin decorated with numerous statues and crowned by a bronze lily. "We Florentine's call this the 'artichoke fountain' because of its shape. Not very nice I suppose, but Italians can be brutally honest to a fault."

From here, the sight opened up on to the large "amphitheatre", adjoined to the hill behind the palace. As they climbed, she pointed out Neptune's fountain. "This one is nicknamed the fork because of his trident."

As they climbed a double staircase, they reached the rampart of the walls built by Michelangelo in 1529, where they quietly enjoyed a view of the Torre al Gall and elegant Florentine manors. As they continued to walk, the path curved around to a magnificent view of Santa Maria del Fiore.

"Here you go. This is the Cathedral of Saint Mary of the Flower—the *Duomo di Firenze*. They began to build her in 1296 but she wasn't structurally completed until 1436, 140 years later. This cathedral has been the seat of the Council of Florence since

1439, heard the preaching's of Savonarola and witnessed the murder of Giuliano di Piero de' Medici in 1478. From this spot renaissance and reformation, revolution and Risorgimento have swept around the city but this Duomo from the middle ages still reigns as its noblest aspect. She's beautiful, isn't she?"

As Klara gazed towards the city, Michael looked only at her. "She is indeed."

CHAPTER FIFTEEN

*F*or the next few weeks Michael found himself busy with work. Although his accommodation had been sorted out his host insisted that he stay on with them, which, to be honest, he was more than happy to do. And if he were perfectly honest, he looked forward to dining with Klara at the end of each day. Her banter and teasing and her intelligence were as enticing as any words of affection, and he found himself feeling lighter and softer in her presence.

He enjoyed the comradeship of James and more than once felt so much at home, that he had entertained the thought of staying and perhaps asking Klara to marry him. The thought became stronger on a daily basis, but the words from the old woman kept ringing in his head. *"She is your soulmate and the only woman you were meant to be with. You need to make a sacrifice, or the consequences will last further into the future than you realize. Better to wait until you meet again."* That evening, fate would take matters into her own hand and would come in the form of a telegram.

The evening began as it usually did, with Michael and James having a brandy before dinner while they waited for Klara to appear and spend a pleasant evening discussing the latest news, politics and books. They had just poured themselves a brandy, when Antonio knocked lightly and entered. "There's an urgent telegram just come for Professor Chamberlain, sir."

Michael looked up from his seat and leaned forward to casually take it from the butler's hand, but his face went white as he read the message.

James looked at him with concern. "Are you all right old chap? Do you need me to top up your Brandy?"

Michael looked lost as if the words on the paper did not make any sense. "Yes, I'm afraid I do. It's my father. There's been an accident. It says he's dead."

James took a deep sigh and put down his drink. "I'm so sorry Michael. Goodness me. How can I help? You will want to make arrangements to return home as soon as possible I expect."

"Yes. I'm afraid I'm not very hungry. Would you mind if I didn't join you for dinner?"

"Of course, of course my boy. Totally understandable, you've had quite the shock. I'll have one of the maids send you up a plate later."

"Thank you, James. I appreciate everything you've done."

Returning to his room, Michael stood by his window for the longest time. He felt as if he were in a trance and couldn't wake up. Feeling in his pocket for the telegram, he read it again, just to make sure that he had read it properly. He had. It took all of his effort to concentrate on what needed to be done. Then forcing himself to move, he began the task of packing his things. Tomorrow he would book his passage on the next available steamer to England. As unreal as all of this felt, he was the man of the family now and decisions would need to be made. The truth though was that somewhere mixed in with all his adult responsibilities, was just a lost little boy.

A little while later, a maid knocked lightly on his door and brought in a plate of cold meats, cheese, bread and white wine.

After placing it on a side table, she gave a little curtsy and left. He continued to work in silence, placing books in his large steamer trunk, taking a small bite of some ham but little more than that. He had no appetite for anything. He could not grasp that his father had died, let alone how. Accident was such a big word and could mean so many things.

Sometime later, when night had settled in and the house was silent, there was a small knock at his bedroom door. Assuming it to be the maid collecting his plate, he remained at the window staring at the rain and wind. But when he turned around, he was surprised to see Klara with a book in her hand. "My uncle wanted you to have his book on reincarnation." He knew his face was a study in pain. It was reflected in her eyes. In an instant she was at his side and tightly embraced him. "Michael, I am so sorry."

It was all he could do not to cry. Biting his lips, he looked deeply into her eyes and as she gazed back up to him, so openly loving him, he kissed her, then kissed her again.

She was in his room and they had crossed the line of no turning back as they hungrily lost themselves in each other's arms. He laid her gently on the bed and knew that neither of them wanted or needed formal courtship rules. She was his as surely as if they had been formally wed and she came willingly.

Soon they were naked, and in the dim light of the gas lamp he gazed down at her milky skin and auburn hair that crowed her face on the pillow and asked her, "Are you sure?"

She nodded. "Surer of anything than I've ever been before."

He kissed her again, slowly, and then dragged his finger across her forehead to move an errant curl. They stayed like that for a few moments looking into each other's eyes. He kissed her lips and neck and slowly moved down to her breasts and ran his tongue over her nipples until she grasped his head and kissed him deeply. He entered her and could barely hold himself back as she gave a little gasp and then moved to his rhythm, arching herself into deep moments of ecstasy.

They fell asleep in each other's arms and in the morning, when he woke, she was gone.

As he was able to get a passage that very day, Michael left with very mixed feelings. He needed to get back and be there for his mother and sister. Be the man his father expected him to be. But a part of his soul would forever be in Florence with the woman he loved.

A LEAP OF FAITH

CHAPTER SIXTEEN

Glastonbury, Present Day

*J*t had been a week since Clara's accident and things had somewhat returned to normal. The bookshop traffic was slow, but that wasn't unusual for this time of year. She had been toying with the idea of creating a website selling vintage "new age" books that were difficult to find as well as items from Glastonbury and opened her laptop to start doing some research. She still couldn't shake the dream she had had about Hamish. It didn't feel like a dream at all. On a whim she typed in Scottish Castles and Dorothea was shocked to get an immediate hit.

There was a Dunbrae Castle that fit her memories and what's more, the Earl of Dunmore's daughter was called Dorothea. This wasn't a dream. She had really been there. She quickly texted Shirley to see if she was next door and free to come over for a minute as she had something amazing to show her.

Two minutes later, Shirley burst through the door causing the little bell to jingle and announce her entrance. Today she had on a long multi-coloured tunic with black leggings.

"What have you found? Is it about the book?"

Clara's eyes were wide with excitement. "No, but look at this. This is it! This is the castle ruins and there really was a Dorothea!"

"It's as I thought then. You had a past life experience and that book is what brought it on."

"But how can that be? The book was written in 1860-something and my dream or memory whatever, was definitely in the 1600's. How could they possibly be connected?"

"My guess is that the Professor who wrote the book may have been Hamish reincarnated in another lifetime and the dedication to Klara was you."

Clara shook her head. "This is getting way too complicated. Wouldn't it be easier if he just walked through the door?"

Shirley laughed. "It would indeed, but unfortunately it doesn't always work that way. Maybe you both had things to work out before you could be together again." She stopped talking for a moment and looked at Clara as if she were trying to make something out. "I think we should try to do a past life regression on you."

"A past life regression? I don't have to bump my head again do I, because it still hurts."

Shirley chuckled and shook her head. "No, no, nothing like that at all. It's kind of like going into a deeper meditation state."

"I don't know. What if I did something terrible in my past life or something bad happened, like I got my head chopped off like Marie Antoinette?"

"My dear, first of all, everyone makes mistakes. You can't change what you did in a past life, but I assure you, you have total control over what you do in this one. As for your second concern, I'll stop you so that you don't emotionally go through a traumatic situation."

"But how will I know if it's not just my imagination?"

"There's no definitive proof what you experience during a regression is factual, but there have been many cases where people have been able to verify facts discovered during a session. You've proved it for yourself finding that Scottish Castle."

"How does it work?"

"Past life regressions provide the opportunity to discover who you may have been in a previous lifetime. It's simply a technique that can help reveal more information about your life or find the source of an attachment in your current life. For instance, your fascination with the name Hamish. For our purposes, we'll explore your karmic path with someone named Hamish who has been with you through multiple incarnations. I'll use guided imagery or hypnosis to regress you to a point in the past. Then I'll ask you questions, and you can tell me what you feel and see. When we're done, I'll take you out of your hypnotic state and bring you back to present time. Easy-peasy. So, what do you think? Want to give it a try?"

"Okay, I'm in as long as you don't turn me into a chicken. When should we do this?"

"Well today's Tuesday and we'll want to set aside a few hours. How about we try for this coming Sunday. Our stores will be closed, Dave will be busy on his latest furniture project and I'll be free."

"That works for me."

"Good. Have a light lunch and come over around one. We'll use my office where I do my readings."

On Sunday, Clara arrived at Shirley and Dave's around one and knocked on the front door. Shortly after, the front door was swung open by Dave, who was dressed in an old Glastonbury Festival T-shirt from the 1990's, with a hammer in his hand and sawdust flecks covering his sparse hair.

"Another project, Dave?"

A large smile spread over his face. "Aye, I've got a lovely old wardrobe from Cornwall that I'm fixing up. Nice piece from the

1800's." He nodded towards the house. "Shirley's in the kitchen love, just making some tea. Go on in. I'm back off to my workshop. No rest for the wicked."

Their home was remodelled from two 16th Century cottages made into one, creating a cozy snug on one side when you first entered, with a small hallway leading into a larger family room and the kitchen on the other. Clara chuckled and greeted Shirley in the hall. Shirley was all smiles as she gave Clara a warm hug. "I thought I heard someone at the front door."

As Clara took off her coat, she said, "Yes, Dave let me in. Looks like he's well into his project."

Shirley smiled. "Bless him, he is indeed. Keeps him busy and out of trouble. Do you want a tea before we start?"

"No, no thanks. I'm too excited."

"Well, come on into my office and we'll have a little chat before we get started." She looked Clara up and down. "You've dressed comfortably—that's good."

Clara laughed. "Shirley, I'm always dressed comfortably." She then stopped and gave her friend a quizzical look. "It just occurred to me that I wear jeans and sweaters because I hated the tight dresses my mother made me wear in the 1600's. I couldn't ride in them. Is that weird?"

"Well, from my point of view it makes perfect sense. Sometimes, specific dislikes that have no basis in your current life may be from a past life event or an emotional response to that event."

Opening the door to her office she ushered Clara in and offered her a chair. Shirley's office was painted a pale blue with white trim around the door and window frames. Dual aspect windows faced the front and side garden, filling the room with light and a pleasant relaxing space. The room smelled of lavender and a faint hint of some kind of incense, nothing too strong but just enough to define that this was a sacred space.

The room was divided into two areas. Two chairs surrounded a side table where her tarot cards lay, wrapped in a square of white silk, while over towards the opposite wall was an old over-stuffed couch where a few pillows and a blanket were placed.

"I'll just put the shades down while you get yourself comfortable on the couch." As she lowered the second shade, she added. "Lay down and put that coverlet over you. You may not feel chilled now, but you'll probably feel it when you're in a more relaxed state."

Clara rearranged the pillows on the couch, choosing a larger one for her head, then got herself comfortable, covering herself with the blanket.

"Just a few points before we get started. First of all, it's important to relax. In order to let your mind wander, deeper into the past, your body must be as relaxed as possible. Don't over analyze or stress about what you might experience. Over analysis prevents you from relaxing completely. Act as an observer during your regression and open your mind to the possibility that what you are seeing might actually be true. Right. Are you comfortable?"

"Yes. I think I am. Hopefully I don't just fall asleep on you."

As Shirley began talking her down into a meditative state, she began to feel more and more relaxed, as if she were sinking into the couch itself. As she was pleasantly floating through space, Shirley's gentle voice was far away. "You are now in a different life, living in another life that you have lived before in another time. You are now reliving that other life that you lived once before in a different time."

Then in an instant she was a young woman giving birth to a baby boy. Although she didn't feel the discomfort of childbirth, she was there just as Shirley said she would be.

"What name can I call you by?" It was Shirley asking her questions, which she found annoying because she was in the middle of having a baby and finding it difficult to concentrate on two things.

"I'm Klara and I'm having a baby. It's a boy!"

"Congratulations, Klara. Can you tell me where you are?"

"I'm in Italy somewhere, but not Florence. I have to have my baby in secret—somewhere in the country because I'm not married."

"How do you feel about that?"

"I love Michael, but he's in England and I am here. I want to be a doctor and that is more important to me than a marriage."

"The father, Michael, does he know?"

"No, I swore my uncle to secrecy. Professor Michael H. Chamberlain II is of the utmost character. He would want to marry me, and I can't leave Florence or my uncle, and he can't leave England. The child will want for nothing and will be raised elsewhere."

"Klara, I'm going to move you forward in time ten years. Can you tell me where you are now?"

Clara felt herself to be very proud. "I'm in Florence of course. I am Italy's first female physician."

"And your son?"

"He is with me. My uncle insisted that he be raised with us and I'm glad that I listened to him. Marcus was able to spend six years with his uncle before he died."

"Marcus?"

"Yes, my son."

"And his father?"

"Michael and I communicate, but too much time has passed. Our lives are too different with commitments on both sides. I know that he still loves me as I do him, but its better this way. He says that he's written a book on reincarnation and has dedicated it to me. It's more of a scholarly account but it is a far more fitting expression of his love for me than flowers. Perhaps in our next life…"

"If I take you to the day you died, where are you?"

"I'm in my bed. I am so, so…cold. My teeth are shivering."

"Are you alone?"

"No, Michael is here. I have written for him to come and he

has. I need him to care for Marcus. Oh, what a mess I've made of things."

"What have you done?"

"Marcus is ten now and they are meeting for the first time. Michael was angry with me at first but he's by my side now, in tears. I realize that I should have done this long ago. But there we have it. I have typhoid and won't live through the day. I'm a physician so I know this to be true. My son will go to live with his father in Oxfordshire and maybe that's for the best. Michael will make sure he grows up into a fine man. I'm feeling very tired."

"Clara, I'm going to be bringing you back now to the present day. Listen to my words and step-by-step I want you to return with me to our time now."

Clara slowly opened her eyes, then quickly closed them again. "That was incredible."

Shirley leaned forward. "Don't get up yet. Give yourself a few minutes."

Clara slowly opened her eyes again and looked around the room. "You were right about the book Shirl. He it wrote for her, but also for me."

"I'll go make us some tea and then we can talk about this some more. Take a few minutes more to just relax. Then we'll chat."

A few minutes later Shirley returned with two steaming mugs of tea. Clara was sitting up but still wrapped in the blanket on the couch, with her legs tucked underneath her.

"How are you dear? You alright?"

"Yes, I'm fine—a little out of it. A little bit sad I guess, but I'm fine."

"I taped our session and took notes, but we'll chat some more now, and I'll write down your thoughts as well. We don't want to miss any little details. Does that sound okay with you?"

"Yes, yes, that's fine."

"Good. When you first arrived, you were having a baby. What do you remember about that?"

"I was in a large room, very expensive was the feeling I got. It felt dark, like it was evening and there were two women there. An older one who seemed to be in charge, the mid-wife I suppose and a younger one who watched from the side. It was a boy, and I was happy about that."

"You said that he would be raised elsewhere."

"I remember saying that. It felt like a baby would be too much trouble for me and besides, I wasn't married, nor did I want to be. More than anything, I wanted to continue my studies to be a physician."

"That's right, you said that you were the first female doctor in Italy."

"I felt very pompous when I said that. Like I had earned the right to be officious. I'm sure I did, but it felt that I had lost some of my sensitivity too. I had studied for so long, fought for my right to be a man's equal, that in the end it felt as if I had lost my femininity in the bargain. I still loved Michael, but we had defined our love through sharing our thoughts through letters, through words, through intellectual exchanges, through our love of learning. Oh, my God, maybe that's why I like books so much!"

"That very well could be. He was there though when you died, wasn't he?"

"Yes, I felt really bad about not telling him he had a son. It must have been difficult for him, meeting his son like that at ten years of age and dealing with me dying at the same time. It would have been the same for Marcus. But in the end, they at least had each other."

"How could he have not known about his son if they wrote letters to each other? Surely she must have mentioned Marcus's name."

"I have the sense that she said he was a ward or something, but never that he was their son."

"I suppose that makes sense. You know, I was thinking that we could try and visit the estate that the furniture came from and see if it's still related to this Professor Chamberlain."

"That would be brilliant."

"I thought you'd like that so I've already hunted down the paperwork and it looks like the estate sale was from a country home in Oxfordshire. Let me do some digging around and see what I can find."

"That sounds perfect."

"Do you have a blank book you can keep by your bed?"

"I do actually. Why?"

"Well sometimes, past life regression can release other memories as well. It could come as a dream, so keep the book and a writing pen by your bedside, just in case. If you do, don't wait until morning—document what you dreamt right away. That way you won't forget anything."

"Okay. Do you think that I've had other past lives with him?"

"I want to say yes, but for some reason we need to explore this Professor first. I'm trusting my intuition and so should you my dear. We'll do this one step at a time."

Clara took the last sips of her tea and took a deep breath. "Do you ever doubt reality? I don't know, how can all this be true?"

"Well, to quote the Bard himself. 'There are more things in heaven and Earth, Horatio, than are dreamt of in your philosophy.' Human knowledge my dear, is a limited thing. The most important lesson from a past life experience is to make sure that you're living this one to the best of your ability."

Clara nodded. "I suppose you're right."

"Go do something relaxing with the rest of your afternoon. Have a nice walk or go shopping or have a bubble bath. It'll help ground yourself back into the here and now. I'll pop into the store tomorrow and check up on you."

Giving her friend a large hug, she said. "I don't know what I'd do without you. Give Dave a hug for me."

"Will do. Now go have a relaxing bubble bath."

CHAPTER SEVENTEEN

*T*he next day Clara was back into the routine of her bookshop, except for a heightened sense of anyone (especially males) walking through the door. Was he Hamish? Would she recognize him? Would he recognize her? It was getting to the point of ridiculousness, and she chided herself on how silly she was being. Picking up the Professor's book, she flipped through a few of the chapters.

If one believes in the existence of God, then the controversial belief in metempsychosis should equally be considered and accepted as fact. It is unfortunate, to the scientific community of spiritualists, skeptics and atheists, that the theory of reincarnation may never be scientifically proven to their satisfaction. This group, of which many of our modern men define their beliefs as such, claim that they cannot offer any proof of the existence of reincarnation and therefore, loudly claim it to be bogus. As such, feelings against the theory of metempsychosis between those who see its possibility and those skeptical of its existence runs high.

In the world of physical science, certain methods must be adopted and followed in order to prove the truth of any given theory. Very recently, Mr. Pasteur published his germ theory which hypothe-

sized and proved that bacteria cause disease. In order to do so, Mr. Pasteur needed to employ the use of a microscope, that without this instrument, germs would be invisible to the naked eye of the observer. If these gentlemen of science deny the existence of germs and refuse to look through the metaphysical microscope, then the experiment cannot be said to be valid, and their opinions are therefore valueless.

Not twenty years ago, cell theory was formulated by the honourable gentlemen, Matthias Schleiden and Theodor Schwann. Although there have been many debates as to the nature and the idea of cells there is a very strong theory that hypothesizes that memories, as well as personality traits, are stored within the cells and organs.

If one were to consider the instinct of herding dogs for example, those who are bred specifically for cows or sheep, one can demonstrate the existence of cellular memories. Indeed, this can also be demonstrated in the avian species flying south etc. It is therefore, not out of the realm of possibilities that homo sapiens can also tap into stored natural and inherited ancestral memories. Many of the reincarnation occurrences that are considered past life recall, can then be logically explained away as ancestor memories.

The soul itself is considered to be a composite of lifetimes of energies that cannot die. Upon the occasion of death, it withdraws from the physical body and unites with the universal cosmic energy. Once the soul enters the new body at birth these memories are imprinted to possibly be awakened through the barometer of our soul—our emotions.

It is common knowledge with those societies who accept reincarnation as a religious dogma rather than a scientific fact, that in many cases, souls become intertwined with each other for many lifetimes. I myself am a convinced believer of metempsychosis and dear readers, I did not go willingly. Initially I was curious but skeptical and designed myself not to be a frivolous believer until I found a scientific explanation for my change of *heart. Thus, the intent of this book is to discuss the scientific merits of such a belief.*

Clara blinked her eyes several times to clear the cobwebs. If the entire book was this dry—she would never get through it.

At that moment Shirley popped her head in through the door. "You'll never guess what! I've just got off the phone with a Susan McClure. She's the great, great grand-daughter of Michael Chamberlain."

"Are you serious?"

"I am indeed. I told her about the book, and she'd love to meet us and see the book for herself. She wasn't aware of it and doesn't want it back by the way, but would love to see it, nonetheless. And here's the best part…"

Clara grinned and gave a little giggle. "Should I give you a drum roll?"

"We're invited for tea next Thursday."

"No! At the estate?"

"Absolutely, at the estate."

CHAPTER EIGHTEEN

*C*lara insisted on driving and picked Shirley up just after one. The entire trip would take around two and a half hours, so she wanted to leave enough time for a small break. Clara gave Shirley an excited grin as they headed north on the A303.

"What did she say about the book again?"

"Well, she seemed pleased that it had found a good home and keen to see it. She said she didn't recall it ever being inventoried and was quite surprised that it had been overlooked as she had emptied out the desk herself."

"Is it a large estate and a listed house and all that?"

"I think it's quite modest, and from the short conversation we had, I understand that it's in need of renovations, hence, her decision to sell off some furniture etc. I think she and her son were hoping to open it up as a wedding venue. As for the house, from what I could glean from the Internet, Chamberlain house is early 18th Century, Baroque-style, built for Alexander Chamberlain, a prominent merchant, in 1720. Susan said that Michael Chamberlain was her great-great-grandfather, so he must have married and had a child at some point.

"Or Marcus is her great-grandfather."

"Very true."

They drove the rest of the way in patches of pleasant silence admiring the view and discussing Shirley's cousin Iris who was on her third husband, despite Shirley's warning of financial concerns. She shook her head in frustration and looked over at the sheep-dotted hills. "Sometimes you just have to let them learn."

About half an hour later, they had reached their destination, and as they drove through the elegant front gates the curved drive led them to the front of the house, where their initial impression was one of fashionable simplicity and unpretentiousness. Chamberlain House was comprised of three stories, with a pedimented centre section standing proudly between the house wings. It was a fine example of early Georgian style. The facade clearly needed some work, along with the grounds. Several areas ringed with trees created the effect that there once may have been more elaborate garden areas. There was certainly a relaxed feeling about it, which perfectly suited its quiet location in the Oxfordshire countryside.

Clara looked around. Chamberlain House appeared to be tucked away in its own little world, in a time warp lost to modernity. If ever there was a place for fairies to live, this would be it. Parking the car, they slowly walked to the front door, taking in the birdsong along with the sense that they had stepped into another era. By the time they had reached the first step towards the entrance, the front door swung open, where they were greeted by an older woman. Although she was more than likely to be in her sixties, she was slim and dressed in jeans, a pink T-shirt and a large, comfortable, unzipped hoodie. Her white hair was pulled back and held by a clip, while her blue eyes and smiling face welcomed them warmly. Clara felt an immediate connection. Her voice held the tiniest of Scottish accents. "Welcome to Chamberlain House. It's Shirley and Clara, isn't it?"

Clara smiled and answered, "Yes."

Shirley took her outstretched hand. "I hope we're not too early."

"No, no not at all. You'll have to excuse my messy clothes though. I was tidying up some of the rooms which haven't seen the light of day, or a dusting I might add, in at least forty years. Come in, come in. I'm so pleased to meet you both. I'm Susan by the way."

In the front entry hall, there was an imperial staircase that split into two in a gentle sweep that rejoined at the landing.

"Wow! That's quite a stunning feature," exclaimed Clara.

"Yes, we're thinking this staircase will do quite nicely for bridal pictures," said Susan. "Would you like a tour of the place before we have some tea?"

"Yes, please, we'd love to," said Shirley.

"My pleasure. It's not very often we get to show off our grand old lady."

Beyond the staircase was a panelled dining room and an impressive gothic library with original Georgian panelling. Many of the panels were not in the best of shape, but there was certainly enough left to be authentically restored. The library itself was a jumble of rare and everyday objects, period furniture and textiles in various states of decay. In the corner was an impressive collection of paint cans, rolled wallpaper and boxes of rags, brushes and loosely folded tarps.

As they followed their hostess through to a large sitting room comfortably furnished in more modern overstuffed couches and chairs, Clara was immediately drawn to several large family portraits of Susan's ancestors. She was immediately struck by one in particular. Following her line of sight, Susan smiled and pointed it out. "That was my great-great-grandfather Michael Chamberlain II. You can see he was quite a handsome man in his day."

Clara felt her knees buckle, for the portrait was identical to the Hamish she knew in the 16th Century. How could this be?

Shirley, who had been watching, was at her side in an instance, "Are you all right? You look a little pale." Grasping her elbow, she steered her towards a chair by a table already setup for tea.

Susan leaned in to help. "Are you okay, dear? Have a seat and I'll be back in a minute with some warm scones and the tea. You'll feel much better I'm sure when we get some food into you."

Shirley smiled back in gratitude. "Can I be of any help?"

"No, no, I won't be but a minute."

After Susan had left the room, Shirley placed her hand on Clara's shoulder and leaned in closer to her. "What happened just now?"

Clara looked towards the portrait in the gilded frame. "It's him, Shirley."

"Well of course it's him. This was his home."

"No, you don't understand. It's Hamish, my Hamish from 16th century Scotland. Could they have been related?"

Shirley let out a long breath of air. "Okay, just relax, have some tea and let me ask some questions."

Susan entered soon after with a tray of tea and scones which were covered by a white napkin on a plate.

"I made these myself, so tuck in while they are warm." She then looked at Clara. "Are you feeling a bit better now? Let me get you some tea." As she poured, she looked at them both. "So, what do you think of Chamberlain House?"

Shirley answered for them both. "You know, it's a beautiful old Georgian style but I have to say, there's a sense of unpretentiousness about it. Does that make sense?"

"I'm so glad you think so. The grounds are quite modest, but there's a lovely terrace at the rear of the house, with steps leading down to water meadows. There are swans there which make it quite special."

"That sounds lovely," replied Clara. "You mentioned your intention for a wedding venue?"

"Yes, but you can see there's quite a bit of renovations to do first and we've somehow got to pay for it. My son is more the driving force behind the idea than I am. I'd be quite happy to sell, but he's keen to keep it in the family. I'm happy to go along and thankfully he has far more energy than I do."

Shirley took a bite of her scone. "These are delicious!"

Susan smiled. "Thank you. It's an old family recipe actually, from my Scottish Granny."

"Your family is originally from Scotland then?"

"Oh, aye, way back in the day on my side and my husband's as well. He was a McClure and although Chamberlain is more English, they were Scottish through and through."

"You mentioned that Michael Chamberlain was your great-great-grandfather."

"Yes, he was indeed. He was a professor at the Bodleian at Oxford. Quite the scholar I understand. Did you bring the book with you?"

"Yes, of course." Clara dug into her purse and pulled out the leather book which she had carefully wrapped in a tea towel. Handing it to Susan, she had a moment of panic that she wouldn't be allowed to keep it.

"This is so kind of you to contact me. As I said on the phone, I had no idea that it existed or even how it was forgotten in the desk drawer." She read the front title, "A Scientific Inquiry into Metempsychosis." She looked back at Clara with a worried look. "I understand that you have a bookstore."

Clara quietly nodded.

"You weren't planning to sell it...in your bookstore I mean... were you?"

Clara looked back at her with alarm. "Absolutely not. No, no. In fact, I feel very connected to this book." She turned to Shirley for back up.

Shirley gently smiled at Clara, then turned to Susan. "To be honest with you we have a bit of a mystery on our hands. I'm a professional psychic..."

"Wait...you're *that* Shirley Forde? I've heard of you. All wonderful things of course. I've heard you're quite good. I'd love to book you here for a weekend when we're up and running... Is that something you'd be interested in?" She looked at Shirley with hopeful eyes and then realized that she had interrupted her mid-sentence. "I'm so sorry, I'm interrupting. Do go on. We can discuss this later."

Shirley grinned. "No worries at all and I'd love to. Anyway, Clara seems to be having some episodes of what appear to be past life memories, in particular, to do with this book. We came to find out more about him."

"Past life experiences. How exciting! I don't know too much but I'm happy to share. I do know that his beliefs were a tad unconventional. He was a history scholar with an interest in different religions, so I'm not entirely surprised at the subject." She opened the dedication page. "To Klara," and then read the rest of the dedication. "Goodness, how romantic of him." At that she turned to Clara and gasped. "Oh, my...it makes sense doesn't it? Klara would be my great-grandfather Marcus's mother. She and the professor never married and when she died, Marcus was brought from Florence to live here. Michael formally acknowledged him as his son. Quite the scandal at the time. Marcus's son, Hamish, was my great-grandfather. My mother Irene was his only surviving child after her brother, my uncle, was killed in World War II. Unfortunately, my father was better at spending money than making it, hence the lack of repairs. When my mother died, she left it to me as I will leave it to my son. Does any of this provide more clarity for you?"

Clara smiled. "I think it provides me some answers and thank you so much for not thinking I'm a lunatic."

Susan patted her hand. "Not at all dear. My husband died a few years ago of cancer and I swear there's times when I feel him around telling me to do this or look out for that. I've always believed that there's more to our lives than just this." Turning to Shirley she continued. "And I meant what I said when I mentioned booking you for a weekend when we're up and running. We've got some money for renovations but not nearly the amount it will take to fix it up properly so we're selling off whatever we can." She looked around the room. "It'll be nice to see the old girl gussied up again."

"You're not doing this on your own I hope."

"No, no. My son and I are in this together. I'm meeting him in Florence next week to pick through the furniture from an old family home there, before it goes up for sale. It's odd that you found the book, because the estate in fact was Klara's. It isn't in the best condition I'm afraid, but it's time we pass it on to someone who has the money to take care of it. After that, we'll return home and it'll be full steam ahead. The plan is to start the initial renos here to make it liveable and then sell the house in London. After that, we'll move in here and get the grand Lady back up and running."

"It sounds like quite the project."

She let out a long sigh. "You have no idea. Right now, I'm sorting through a herd of chairs to be restored."

Shirley perked up. "My husband restores furniture."

"Does he? Maybe he can give me some tips then because I have no idea what I'm doing. I was thinking of taking a class."

"Tell you what, when you and your son get back, why don't we come up for a weekend and give you a hand. Dave can show you how it's done first hand."

"How very kind of you. That would be brilliant. Are you sure?"

"Absolutely, we'd be happy to help. Keep in touch, and just let us know when it would be convenient."

"Well, I'll gratefully take you up on that. My expectation is that we'll be back by the beginning of April."

"Excellent. We'll consider it a date. Well, we have a long drive ahead and I expect you've got a full afternoon of chores, so we won't delay you any longer."

"The pleasure has been all mine, I assure you. I quite feel like I've made some very good friends."

"You know, I've got a very good feeling about this place."

"Have you really? I sometimes think we're quite mad taking this on."

Taking Clara's hand, she looked deeply into her eyes. "Thank you so much for bringing the book here and showing it to me. I have the oddest feeling that it was always meant to be yours. And do come back and visit. You'll always be welcome."

CHAPTER NINETEEN

*L*ife returned to normal after their visit, which was predominantly books for Clara, and meant that Michael Chamberlain took a back seat to everything involved in selling books, especially inventory, shipments, pricing and stacking. Valentine's Day was made special by Shirley and Dave, who walked in with a lovely bouquet of flowers and a bottle of wine. The card simply read, "To the love of my life, Hamish." After they had dutifully finished the wine, she had tucked the card by the cash register, which brought a smile to her face whenever she saw it. She had also made one big decision lately, which she was thrilled about. On their drive back, Clara and Shirley had discussed the idea of starting a meditation group in the store every Wednesday evening. Shirley had been asked several times to start one, and using the bookstore was a brilliant solution for a venue. The store would be closed, books would be recommended and would provide them both with a little extra income.

The group had started the week before and was quite promising. So far, they were a group of eight. There were the Four Musketeers, all older ladies in their fifties and sixties, Bryan and Scott, a gay couple in their thirties, Bethany, a buxom blonde in her early twenties and Edward Bronson, a proper English gentleman if ever there was one, who had the Four Musketeers all atwitter during break. Shirley had called earlier to say that tonight they were expecting two more, which brought the group to a respectable ten, not counting her and Shirley.

Clara counted the folded wooden chairs stacked on the second floor to ensure that there would be enough seats and checked the fridge for cream and milk. Shirley had brought some old mugs in from home and between them they had set up the second floor to be a bit cozier, and to ensure that all the drinks would remain on that level. Satisfied that all was well, Clara fixed herself some tea and looked through the latest catalogue of new releases from her supplier. She was just about to take some notes on potential stock when Shirley burst through the door.

"Hallooo, Clara?"

Dressed in a deep purple tunic with three strings of long beads of various polished stones, she certainly looked the part of the leader of a meditation group. Today, she was sporting a violet streak in her short white hair. "I got an email this morning from Susan. She's back and wondering whether we'd like to come up for the mid-April Bank Holiday. She says the plumbing will be sorted out by then and if we don't mind roughing it a bit, we could make a weekend out of it."

"That sounds like fun actually. I can get my neighbour's daughter to take care of Lucy for me and I'm sure your niece Ellie will be fine on her own looking after the bookshop." Ellie was a tall, slender, seventeen-year-old, and sported shocking pink and purple streaks down each side of her long blonde hair. Clara recognized her as someone who had already been to the shop before and familiar with the store's genre and layout.

"What about you and Dave. Does that weekend work for you?"

"Are you kidding? Dave is already making a list of what tools to pack. Stuck on an old estate with antique furniture is his dream come true. He may never leave."

They both laughed and commenced setting out the chairs.

Shirley patted the back of the chair she had just put down. "I'll tell her it's a go then."

"It'll be fun, although I'm not sure how much help I'll be with refurnishing."

The tinkling bell at the front door indicated that their group had started to arrive, but when she hurried downstairs, she was intrigued to see a handsome man around her age holding the door open for a well-dressed older woman. Realizing she hadn't put the closed sign out in the window she walked towards them expecting to explain that the store was closed but the man spoke first. "Hello, we're here for the meditation group. This is my mother Margaret and I'm Robert."

A little bit surprised at their response, Clara hesitated for a moment. "Welcome. I'm Clara, and somewhere up there is Shirley, who leads the group. I'm so glad you could make it." Pointing towards the steps she ushered them up to the second level. "We're just setting up, but please come up and have a seat. I've got some stands upstairs to hang up your coats."

As she climbed the stairs behind them, Clara couldn't help but feel a tingle of excitement over such a handsome addition to their group. As they reached the second level, Shirley, whose head was currently in the refrigerator, popped her head back out and looked towards the pair with a large smile. "Margaret Evans is that you? Goodness I didn't recognize you. Aren't you a sight for sore eyes." Walking towards her she reached out for a big hug. Then still holding Margaret's hands at arms-length looked admiringly at her son. "This cannot possibly be young Robert?"

"I'm afraid it is." Margaret looked at her tall, handsome son with pride, while an embarrassed "young Robert" rolled his eyes and grinned at Clara. Shirley looked at Clara not realizing that small fireworks were going off inside her friend's tummy. "Margaret and I went to school together and the last time I saw this young man, he must have been six or seven."

"It's certainly been a while, Shirley."

"I didn't recognize your name when you booked."

"After Robert's father passed away, I remarried. It's Henderson now."

"We are going to have to make a point of catching up after tonight. I'm surprised to see you here tonight though. Is everything alright?"

At that moment the Four Musketeers, as well as Bryan and Scott arrived, and Clara reluctantly went back downstairs to greet them.

As hard as she tried to listen in on the conversation upstairs the boisterous ladies made it impossible to hear anything apart from their back and forth chatter. Bryan hugged her soundly while Scott raved about the violet hair colour on one of the Musketeers. As the group made their way upstairs, she could hear introductions being made while she waited for the last two to arrive. Not long after, Bethany arrived and a minute later Edward. At last, she could lock the door and head back upstairs.

Joining the group, she was not surprised to see that Bethany had chosen a seat next to Robert. This meant she was forced to sit in a chair three seats away, making it entirely difficult to "accidently" catch his eye. This also meant that Robert would be holding hands with a hot twenty-something with blonde hair, blue eyes, and big tits that were currently being shown off in their full glory due to a form fitting, low cut, blue sweater. Clara smiled while Shirley began to talk, but inside she was comparing her old stretched grey sweater, her messy hair clipped up in what could only resemble a bird's nest and her plain, no make-up face. She didn't stand a chance. Why oh, why, did she not bother to try harder?

Snapping back to the present, everyone was in the process of holding hands and she grasped the hands of Edward on one side and Bryan on the other. Shirley began the meditation with a prayer and in low, dulcet tones, guided everyone through the meditative process. As Clara closed her eyes and breathed deeply, she too became more relaxed and softer around the edges.

Suddenly, Edward's voice boomed and his grasp on her hand

tightened. "I have someone here with me that wishes to make himself known."

Shirley's voice took over. "Welcome friend. By what name should we call you?"

Edward's voice was firm. "Henry."

Clara could feel her face pale. "Grandad?"

"He's saying the message is for his little fairy."

Clara could not contain her tears. "He says that your mom and dad are with him and they are all so proud." By this time, Clara's tears flowed down her cheeks in hot salty rivulets onto her sweatshirt.

"He's saying something that I can't make out, but essentially, that *it's his turn to find you.*"

Clara had a clear memory of playing hide and seek in the shop and taking turns with who found whom. What clearer message could he give that it was indeed her grandfather. Wiping her cheeks with the back of her hand, she whispered, "I miss you too Grandad. Give mom and dad a hug for me."

Edward relaxed and said that "he" was gone now and the group went silent. Shirley guided the session into a meditation on self-healing and then finally prayers for those in need. As they ended the meditation and coasted back to the here and now, Clara felt a lump in her throat at what had just transpired. Shirley guided the group to open their eyes briefly then close them again to reflect on their inner feelings. Clara felt sad. Then realised that her face was blotchy, streaked with tears and she desperately needed to blow her nose. By the time the group had slowly begun to stand up and stretch, Clara had already grabbed a tissue from a nearby table and headed downstairs to clear her sinuses. She shouldn't have been surprised that her Grandad had come through, after all it was his store, but the intensity of remembering the security of his love and her need to be loved was overwhelming.

As she climbed the stairs back to the group, Robert was there at the top looking at her. "You okay?"

Unsure of whether she would start crying again, she bit her lip while attempting to smile. "I'm okay. It just took me by surprise is all."

"I can imagine. My mother and I are here because of her husband Frank. My stepfather died last year, and she's been having dreams that he's trying to tell her something. She was hoping that Shirley could help and I'm here for support."

Clara nodded. "Well, if anyone can, Shirley can. I'm sorry, I'd like to chat more, but I need to help Shirley with the tea and cookies."

"Of course, of course, please don't let me get in the way."

As Clara was helping Shirley put out the cookies, her friend gave her a quick pat on the back. "You all right?"

"Yes. I forgot how much I miss him."

"We'll chat about it later." Looking off towards Robert, she nodded in his direction. "He's a bit of a dish, isn't he? And a lawyer."

"And don't think Bethany hasn't noticed." As if on cue, she was suddenly beside him, tossing her hair and giggling at something Scott had just whispered in her ear. What was very odd though, was that during her animated and obvious attempt to flirt with Robert, he looked up and straight back at Clara with the faintest of smiles, as if they shared an understanding.

CHAPTER TWENTY

*T*he April Bank Holiday weekend arrived far sooner than she was ready for. A shipment of books had arrived the day before and she was anxious to cross-reference her list, get them into the system, then priced and stocked on the shelves. Going away for the weekend was the last thing on Clara's mind. Over the past month and a half, Margaret had attended the next two meditation groups alone, explaining that her son Robert had a big case that he was working on and wouldn't be joining her for a while. As an aside, she commented that it really wasn't his "thing" anyway. Bethany pouted, but by the following week had brought along a musician that she had just met. She was convinced that she and Forest were soul mates, or at least would be, Shirley commented to Clara, until someone better came along.

Bryan and Scott were regularly bringing homemade sweet treats every week, along with vegan snacks for Bethany. And lastly Edward, obviously charmed by the attentions of the Four Musketeers, was regularly regaling the ladies with stories of his by-gone travel days in Europe. He reminded Clara of a strutting rooster in a hen house. However, as much as she wanted to stay and get work done, she *had* promised to help out, and if she were being really honest with herself, she knew the break would do her good. After tidying up her office, she pulled down the shades, put up the closed sign, set the alarm, and locked the doors.

～

Dave and Shirley, who had insisted on driving in their larger CRV, picked her up at her home a few hours later. Dave, with his tools in the back, had made a variety of classic music tapes from the sixties, while Shirley had sorted out a cooler of cut veggies, with little plastic containers of humous and quartered ham sandwiches. They were all set for their adventure and sang along to House of the Rising Sun, Brown-eyed Girl, The Supremes, The Beatles and the Rolling Stones. Clara could not remember when she had sung herself hoarse or laughed so loud. *Had she ever?*

Shirley reached behind and grabbed her hand. "I'm so glad you're coming this weekend."

Giving her a little squeeze back, she smiled warmly. "Me too."

They arrived several hours later, just as it was approaching dusk, and as they drove down the winding drive, Chamberlain House seemed to be quietly awaiting their arrival. The front entryway was lit up and as they parked, Susan was once again there to warmly greet them. "Helloo, helloo! You've arrived!"

As she gave Shirley and Clara each a warm hug, she stopped short at Dave. "Hello there, you must be the clever man who's going to teach me how to sort out our chairs. I'm Susan."

"Hello, I'm David, but everyone calls me Dave, and yes, we'll give it a good shot."

"Well, come on in and we'll get you all sorted out. I can't thank you enough for helping me with this. I'm afraid the weekend will be a bit full-on, but I've got lots of good food and wine to keep you happy. I might add, the plumbers were here last weekend, so you'll have good strong water pressure for showers and running toilets."

"It sounds like fun."

"Well, it's a start. Right, let's get you all settled first."

"Shirley and Dave, I've tidied up the blue room for you both. You'll be up the stairs and it's the first room to your right. Clara, I've given you the green room – second door to your left. You're going to love the bathtub dear. It's a pretty little room, or rather it will be when it's been repainted and, and, and… Point is, it has a very pretty bathtub and toilet that works and it's been cleaned."

Clara laughed as Susan led them upstairs and showed them their rooms. Leaving Clara to last, she gave her a hug before opening her bedroom door. "You're all so very kind to help me like this."

As the door opened, Clara gave a little gasp. It was classic Georgian romance. A series of faded light green panels trimmed in white covered the walls, while ornate crown mouldings bordered the ceilings. A gorgeous old chandelier that needed some love, hung in the centre of the room. The bed was a delicately carved oak four poster, and although it lacked the canopy above, the thick white duvet and bolstered pillows promised a luxurious sleep tonight. "It's absolutely beautiful!"

"I'm so glad you like it, Clara. Check out this bathtub." Clara followed her into the en-suite where a large gleaming copper tub surrounded in an ornate floral grill took centre stage. "Isn't that something?"

"Oh, my goodness. Well, I know what I'll be doing later."

"Make sure you do. It's quite the lap of luxury that tub. Now, when you've freshened up come on downstairs and we'll start our weekend off with a proper glass of wine and a catch-up."

"You don't have to twist my arm."

Twenty minutes later she joined them all in the same room where they had had tea the last time they had visited. Dave was already busy explaining something to Susan, presumably regarding the panelling he was pointing at. As she entered the room, Shirley, with a quick smile, sauntered over and gave her a hug. "He's in his element now."

Clara giggled. "There'll be no stopping him I'm afraid."

As they both stood back and watched in amusement, Dave had already moved on to the benefits of traditional lime plastering. After a few minutes, Shirley, feeling a little pity for Susan, interrupted. "Dave, there's plenty of time to tutor her on the finer points of plastering. Come and join us. Susan, will your son be joining us this weekend?"

"Sadly no. We've had an offer on the Florence villa, so he's stayed on to complete the sale and ensure the rest of the shipment of antiques gets sent safely back here."

"That's a shame. We were looking forward to meeting him."

"And he you. He's quite keen on doing some of the work himself."

"Does he do woodworking?"

"Shay? Goodness no. He's in business. But he's never been one to shy away from hard work, I'll grant him that."

Looking at the three of them, Susan gave them all a big grin and nodded towards the four empty wine glasses and a bottle of wine. "I brought out a bottle of red, but I have a nice Riesling in the fridge or prosecco if you prefer."

After everyone agreed that the red was fine, she poured four glasses and handed one to each of them. "Well, let me wish you all a warm welcome, cheers to new friendships and a mighty thank you for helping me out."

As they clinked glasses, Susan smiled warmly at Clara and as she smiled back, she was glad she had come. Clara liked her.

Despite Susan's protests, dinner was a group effort, hands-on affair, with Shirley and Clara setting the table and Dave carrying in the hot plates of roast chicken, bacon and leek pie, mashed potatoes and mixed greens. Later, Clara cleared the plates while Susan brought in the desert of a Bakewell tart with ice cream.

Patting his tummy, Dave leaned back and contentedly groaned. "That was absolutely crack on delicious."

It wasn't a late night and the conversation soon faded a few hours later. So, with the promise of an early morning ahead, Clara afforded herself the luxury of a deep, hot, bubble bath, a cozy bed and a dreamless night sleep.

~

The next morning, she found everyone up and already in the kitchen discussing the plans for the day. Susan looked up as Clara walked into the room. "Oh, Clara, how did you sleep, dear?"

"Very well, thank you. The room was wonderful. I can't remember the last time I slept so soundly."

"I'm so glad to hear it. There's coffee and tea over on the side counter there, and I've got some croissants, cereal or yogurt and fresh fruit if you like."

"I'll start with a tea for now, thanks."

"Shirley, Dave and I are just about to get started and have a look at the chairs. I'm wondering though if you could do me a huge favour?"

"Of course!"

"In the library, there's a large steamer trunk we brought back with us from the villa in Florence. Towards the end, Shay was just packing everything, everywhere – you know how men can be. Anyway, there's a load of books and who knows what else. It would be a huge favour if you could sort through the books and whatever items are there. We'll need to catalogue everything and I figured you, with your bookstore inventory expertise, would be the perfect person."

"I'd love to, although I'm sure Dave will be missing my 'expertise' on sanding."

Dave was quick to respond. "You're right on that count. I completely missed that you had any sanding expertise at all."

Shirley chuckled and slapped her husband on the arm who immediately winced, rubbed the spot that she hit and declared spousal abuse.

Clara grinned back as she finished her tea.

Susan chuckled at Shirley. "I can see you've got your hands full with that one."

Shirley shook her head and gave her a mock look that showed she appreciated her support. "I do indeed."

"The library's down the hall to the left of the stairs and I've put out some paper and pens for you. If you need anything else, we'll be in the ballroom at the end. There's a list of what each box *should* contain and if you could check off the list to make sure they've arrived in one piece that would be wonderful."

After eating a small croissant and finishing her tea, Clara headed in the direction that Susan had indicated. She could hear Dave discussing the cost of upholstering a certain chair from across the hall and chuckled to herself. As she entered the library she smiled as the familiar scent of chocolate and earth, smoke and coffee prickled her nose. This was the smell she loved -old books infused with the passage of time.

Georgian libraries typically provided estate owners an opportunity to display their wealth, and in this case the effect was clearly achieved. Bookshelves stacked with hundreds of leather-bound books lined the walls. Two ladders on long brass rails led her eye to a soaring ceiling and a series of tall windows that let in the morning sunlight. A few small tables and comfortable chairs were set near a large white fireplace and a pianoforte. A deep red, well-worn Turkish carpet covered the floor, while two large globes were huddled in the corner. A large antique desk faced the door.

As she wandered around, a deep silence tugged at her soul and she marvelled at the immense collection of leather-bound books. In the days of circulating libraries, these books would have been expensive and considered a luxury. There was no question that Michael Chamberlain was a professor and fellow lover of books. It wasn't hard to envision him, in his deep blue velvet *robe de chambre* smoking a cigar and reading these very books.

Near the windows were two large open crates containing several sealed boxes. Looking around for a cutting knife, she found it on a nearby table, along with a pad of paper, a pen and a list of what the boxes contained. Her job would be to check each item off the list as she unpacked it. Pleased with the task that lay ahead, she carefully lifted the first box onto the desk and slid the knife through the packing tape. Inside were several undiscernible items wrapped in bubble wrap and more tape. No wonder Susan needed help. This was clearly going to take a while.

The first two pieces were exquisite apothecary vases. One in cobalt blue and the other in green with an ornate guild front. She easily found them on the list and checked them off as arrived and undamaged. As she slowly went through piece by piece, she felt her excitement rise as each item was released from its plastic binding. Lovingly she held each item as if she were seeing things that she had not seen for a long time. There was an overwhelming sense that she was connecting with her things once again. *How was this possible?*

She opened the next item and the next, all with a sense that she had seen them, held them, owned them all before. A small silver clock, made in Italy in the first half of the 19th Century. There was a marble bust of a woman, noted on the list as an 18th Century copy of the original in the Uffizi. A chiseled silver goblet, crystal jars with silver lids embossed with daisies, and an amazing painted fan marked down as early 18th Century by Pietro Penna. A gilded bronze clock and candelabras with painted porcelain inserts from France. Pottery, plates, tea sets, small pictures and a carved lion door knocker that she recognized even before she touched it, and books, lots of leather-bound books in English and Italian. Finally, a lady's toilet set with a brush, mirror and comb. It was this more than anything else that made her react. There was something so familiar about the brush that it startled her. Slowly turning the brush over she found what she knew would be there. A monogram engraved on the silver... K. B. - Klara Brydon.

CHAPTER TWENTY-ONE

*L*ater that afternoon, Susan walked into the library to see how Clara was coming along. She was delighted with her progress as almost all the boxes had been unpacked and their contents organized and inventoried in a database.

"I can see you have done this more than once. I knew you were the right one for the job!"

Clara chuckled. "After growing up in a bookstore, I think it comes naturally."

"I suppose it does. Shirley told me about your parents and being raised by your grandfather in his bookshop. Did you miss having parents?"

Before Clara could open her mouth to answer, Susan, clearly flustered with herself carried on. "Goodness, there I go again, being a busybody. I'm so sorry, you don't have to answer that question."

"No, no it's fine. I think that I missed the experience of having parents like all my friends, but there was never a point that I didn't feel loved. My grandad did his best to fill all of those roles for me. I do think though that once I became a teenager and certainly an adult, I missed the opportunity to know them. I would like to have a memory of my mother's hug or sitting on my father's knee, something more substantial than a vague foggy memory of their faces."

Susan, clearly moved by her words, took a step closer and held out her arms. "I'm so sorry about your parents, but I'm pleased to know you were well cared for. You know, I've always wanted a daughter, but it wasn't in the cards. Will a big motherly hug from me do for now?" As Susan wrapped her arms around her and held her close for a few minutes, and in that warm embrace, Clara felt her mother's love. But more than that, she felt at home.

Taking a step back, Susan slid her hands down to Clara's arms and looked back at her from an arms-length. "Tell you what, I could use some help in the kitchen for dinner if you're up to it."

Clara smiled back warmly. "I'd love to. Although I'm not sure how much help I'll be. I've never really learned to cook."

Susan patted her arms twice and took charge. "Well now, that's something we change today. Everyone should know how to cook at least one dish. Leave the rest of this for tomorrow and let's go have some fun in the kitchen, shall we?"

"I'm in your capable hands."

Following her through the hallway they entered a bright and spacious kitchen that had obviously been seriously updated since it's Georgian roots. It was ultra-modern with clean white marble counters, a large range, appliances, splashes of green tiles and copper pots everywhere. Seeing Clara's amazed face, Susan chuckled as they walked in. "Not very traditional I admit, but with what we want to do here, there was no way I was going to fiddle with antique stoves and a lack of counter space. I've treated myself to all the mod cons we could afford. What do you think?"

"I think it's the most impressive kitchen I've ever been in."

"I think so too. Let's get started, shall we? Tonight's menu is roast fillet of salmon with tomato, chili, garlic, capers, green beans and linguine. And for dessert, blackberry and pear crumble."

"It sounds delicious and complicated. You direct and I'll do my best not to mess it up."

"No worries, it's quite an easy dish to prepare. I only have one rule."

Clara smiled, her eyebrows raised. "And that is?"

"I never cook dinner without a glass of wine. Will you join me?"

"Well, if I'm going to learn to cook properly, I think it's important for me to follow the head chef's rules, don't you?"

Susan gave a nod as she headed to her wine fridge. "Good girl. I can see you and I are going to get along just fine."

After a brief little toast to cooking, Susan asked Clara to wash all the vegetables and fruit as she poked around in the pantry and cupboards for some bowls and utensils. They chatted amiably about Susan's plans for landscaping the grounds outside.

After the initial prep, Susan then turned her attention towards the meal. "We'll start with the dessert first. I always like to measure out all my ingredients first and have everything ready to go before I actually start. I know it adds to the washing up, but then I don't miss any steps. I've pulled out some little bowls, so while I measure out the flour and sugar, how about you shell these pistachios and roughly chop them up. We'll need 85g, so you can use this little scale over here."

As Clara split the hard shells away from the pistachio nuts, she quietly thought how this is what it would have felt like to have a mother. Chopping away at the nuts, she realized that the simple act of casual conversation with a female friend, while sipping wine and preparing a dinner was something she had totally missed out on. More importantly, this was something she wanted to do more of. Lost in thought, she didn't hear Susan's question and had to ask her to repeat it.

"I was saying that you may want to weigh those pistachios. I suspect that you've got more than enough right now."

"Oh goodness. I wasn't sure how much 85g was."

"I'm guessing you've got around a 100g there, but no worries.

Weigh out the 85g and we'll set aside the extra. It'll get used no matter what. After that, I'll get you to peel and cube those four pears."

"Now that I can manage."

Susan took another sip of wine before weighing out a large bowl of blackberries. "You know I meant what I said a while ago. I always wanted a daughter. I always imagined that she and I would be sharing a glass of wine, sharing a laugh while cooking together in the kitchen. I'm so glad you were able to come this weekend. It's a bit of a treat for me. I hope I didn't interrupt any plans with a boyfriend. He could have joined us—I wouldn't have minded."

Clara stopped peeling for a moment to answer. "No boyfriend. Sadly, I seem to be too busy or too boring for most men I'm afraid."

"Well, I find that very hard to believe. But don't you worry, there'll be someone who will love you for exactly who you are. That I'm certain of."

"I hope so. I'd like to think there's someone special in my future. Children too."

"Well, I'll keep my eye out for a knight in shining armour for you, and when Mr. Right does arrive, you'll be having your wedding here. Oh! That idea deserves a 'cheers'!"

As they clinked glasses, Susan giggled. "We'll plan it together!"

They spent the next few hours laughing, chatting and cooking, and by the time dinner was ready Clara felt as if she had known Susan forever. She also knew that she was exactly the kind of mother that she wanted to be with her own daughter.

~

After dinner, which everyone praised as delicious, Shirley and Dave insisted on washing up as Susan and Clara sat back and enjoyed another glass of wine. Susan was all smiles at a harmless comment that Dave had made at Shirley's expense and her quick-witted retort. "You two remind me of me and my husband. My God, that man could make me laugh. I can't remember when I've had such an enjoyable weekend. I am so pleased that you all came, and I'll be sorry to see you go. In fact, I've got a brilliant idea that I will not take no for an answer. My son and I are planning on having a grand gala event this New Year's Eve and I want you to join us. And before you say no – this is my thank you gift to you. It would mean a lot to me, so say yes. We're thinking of a 1940's theme. It'll be so much fun!"

Shirley, Dave and Clara took only a moment to look at each other before giving her a resounding, "Yes!"

To seal the deal, Susan raised her glass and nodded to them all to do the same. "To New Years' Eve, wonderful new beginnings and friendships."

∼

The next day, as Clara was packing her overnight bag to leave, there was a small knock at her door. In the middle of folding a sweater, she quickly turned around and answered. "Come in."

The door opened and Susan popped her head inside. "I'm sorry to interrupt dear but I wanted to give you something." In her hand was a small red box.

"How sweet of you."

She held out the box to Clara, gave a little smile and nodded for her to open it.

Clara lifted the lid and in awe, placed her hand to her chest. Inside was a small 19th Century figurine of a little girl and her mother, *and she felt an overwhelming certainty that she had seen this figurine before.*

LOVE IS A LEAP

CHAPTER TWENTY-TWO

*T*hey arrived back home late in the afternoon, and while Clara unpacked and sorted out the laundry to be done, Lucy did her usual figure eights around her ankles. Lucy would need a lot of attention tonight in order for Clara to be forgiven for leaving her alone for the weekend. After a light dinner, she poured herself a small glass of wine and placed the figurine on the shelf with her mother's keepsakes. She smiled. It felt as if it belonged there, belonged to her not just now, but in the past. *Clearly it had been Klara's.* Sitting in the armchair in front of the fire, with Lucy on her lap, she thought back over the weekend.

Chamberlain House would be beautiful when the renovations were completed, and she really had enjoyed herself and had loved spending time with Susan. It wasn't long before the warmth of the fire worked its magic and she slowly dozed off into a deep sleep. As she slumbered, memories slowly crept out from the dark recesses of her mind, tugging at the threads of her soul. One by one the strands edged closer and closer, piecing together little memories, until a heartbeat later, her dreams took her to another time, to another place, and to another person.

~

The man's voice was sharp, urgent. "Nurse, over here!"

Kathleen swung her flashlight over to a doctor in combat fatigues examining a wounded soldier who was sitting on the edge of a cot. She rushed to his side, wearing her helmet and carrying a full pack containing musette bags, gas masks and canteen belts. Only her Red Cross arm band and lack of weapon distinguished her from the fighting troops. The abandoned building situated between an ammunition dump and an airfield, both primary targets for German bombers, was not the most ideal location for a makeshift hospital. A high-explosive bomb had already destroyed the east side of the building, penetrating a concrete wall, and the considerable damage had forced their commanding officer to order them to evacuate to a safer part of the building. It was dark and cold. There was a rush to evacuate as many of the wounded as they could, before this part of the building collapsed and they were buried in the rubble.

Kathleen, three other combat nurses, and a handful of Doctor's were currently in the process of evaluating over fifty soldiers who lay on the concrete floor in pools of blood. Those too injured or who could not be moved would need to stay with the nurses. Kathleen already knew she would be one of the ones to stay behind. She looked around as the young men cried out in pain and fear. The sounds of enemy aircraft, artillery guns and bombs accompanied their cries. She didn't blame them. She was as scared as they were, but she had a job to do. Many of them were only boys, eighteen or nineteen years old. They were hurt, scared and just wanted to go home. Her heart reached out to every one of them. Too many of these kids would never see home again.

With no electricity or running water, the only medical supplies available were those the nurses had brought themselves. Doctors operated under flashlights held by nurses and enlisted men. Kathleen dispensed what comfort she could, although the only sedatives available were the ones that she had carried with her. As she made her way towards the corner to assess a young officer, a sudden intense blast threw her forward. Her next moments consisted of coughing, dust, darkness, disorientation and excruciating pain. An eerie silence followed the muffled agonizing screams of trapped patients and medical staff. She remembered her spare flashlight, and struggled to free it from a side pocket in her pack, but every movement sent a surging pain to her leg. Finally securing it, she shone her light to access her situation. Although it appeared that she had missed the majority of the avalanche of cement and rubble, part of the wall had splintered and fell on top of her, pinning her legs to the floor, entombing herself and the wounded soldier she had been about to access. It didn't look good. The amount of blood indicated a deep gash and she was more than aware that the enormous cement block pinning her down was likely saving her from bleeding out. It was too large and heavy for her to move on her own and even if she could, it was highly unlikely that she would have been able to save the leg or her life.

The bloody bandages over the soldier's chest indicated he was not in any better shape. He appeared to be in his late twenties, dark hair and handsome, but the fact that the light didn't register on his face was a sure indication that he was blind as well as seriously injured.

Shouting until she had no more strength left, her voice became hoarse. No one came. No one would. Slowly and frighteningly, the dull screams of the others fell silent. As a combat nurse, it wasn't hard to figure out that death robbed many of their voices, while injury and exhaustion made it impossible for others to muster the strength to respond.

She turned off the light to save the battery and thought about home. About how difficult it would be for her mum to get the telegram after already losing two sons.

From the darkness, the soldier started to cough over and over again, then weakly spoke. "What's happened?"

"The building's been bombed, and it's collapsed. We seem to be trapped in a lot of rubble and my leg is pinned under a large chunk of cement. I'm afraid it doesn't look very good."

"Doesn't sound very promising."

Kathleen coughed from the dust and was feeling a little light-headed. "I wish I had something more positive to tell you, or at least be of more help."

"I kind of figured when I was brought in here that I wasn't walking out. Can I ask your name?"

"Nurse Morgan."

"Sounds a bit formal for someone who I may die alongside with. What's your real name Nurse Morgan?"

She smiled to herself. There didn't seem to be much sense in following protocols now. "Kathleen."

"Kathleen Morgan. You have a nice voice, Kathleen. I'm Robert, but my mates call me Bobby. Are you as pretty as your voice?"

Kathleen chuckled despite the pain. "Are you always such a charmer?"

He sounded raspy like he was trying to breathe through the pain. "Just to the pretty ones, Kathleen. From around Bristol area, right?"

"I am, and you're from around Cornwall I'm guessing."

"You've got a keen ear. Pretty and smart. If I wasn't so busted up I'd give your fella a run for his money."

"No boyfriend I'm afraid. Nor husband."

"I can't believe that—pretty girl like you." She could hear him wince. "How long have you been in France?"

"Not long. Six months now I think, but feels like forever."

"Brave girl to be here at the front."

"I'm not sure how brave I am. I just wanted to make a difference and be where my nursing skills would be needed the most. I admit though, I hadn't counted on the mud, the snow and draughty tents. What about you, Bobby?"

"Signed up with my older brother as soon as I could. We thought it would be an adventure—teach those Jerrys a lesson y' know? Turned out to be a different kind of adventure though. We lost Thomas to sniper fire a few months back and now I'm looking a little worse for wear. It's gonna kill me mum to lose us both."

Searching her mind for questions to keep him awake and talking, Kathleen pursed her lips and took a deep breath. "We'll get out of this, you'll see. Just hold on and don't lose hope."

"Don't be putting on a brave front for me, Kathleen. What day is it anyway?"

She closed her eyes and chuckled. "New Year's Eve, Bobby. New Year's Eve 1942."

"No kiddin'? You know I always thought I'd meet the woman I was meant to marry on New Year's. Well, being that neither of us is likely to make it out of here alive, I say in our next life we agree to meet under better circumstances, fall madly in love and live happily ever after."

Kathleen sighed. It was just her luck to meet Mr. Right on the day they were both likely to die. "I'd like that. And where do you suppose we should we meet?"

"Well, considering the date, I'd say a fancy New Year's Eve dance would be appropriate."

Her head was beginning to swim. "Sounds lovely. And how will I recognize you?"

"No need. I'll find you."

Kathleen smiled. "And how do you plan on recognizing me?"

"Easy, you'll be the most beautiful woman in the room and wearing a strapless red dress. A real knockout, and every man in the place will be envious of seeing you in my arms."

"You're a charmer, Bobby, but I'm glad you're here with me."

Suddenly, his breathing became laboured, and he struggled to cough. "Kathleen...I'm not going to last much longer. If you get out...tell my mum I'm sorry."

"I will."

"And Kathleen?"

"Don't talk, Bobby, you need to conserve your strength."

"We'll dance in our next life, won't we?"

There was a gurgling sound, a sudden whoosh of air and he was silent.

She leaned her head back and closed her eyes as hot tears trickled down her cheeks. "In my red dress, I promise."

Clara woke up with a start, disoriented as to where she was. Lucy, annoyed with the interruption, jumped off of her lap and found a comfortable place to curl up to by the fireplace. Still a little shaken, she stared into the fire. What had just happened? The dream was uncomfortably real and felt as if she had actually been there—died there. Feeling raw from the experience, she remembered what Shirley had suggested and grabbed her journal to write down the details. She would discuss this with her friend tomorrow.

The next day, when Shirley popped into the bookshop, she was all smiles. Apparently, Robert would be joining them this coming Wednesday, but she was surprised by Clara's face.

"I thought you'd be happy that he's coming."

"It's not that at all, Shirley. It's happened again. I had a weird intense dream about being a combat nurse in World War II. But it was different from a typical dream where there's a beginning, middle and end. In my dream, I suddenly found myself in the middle of a scene as though I'd stepped into a movie on the big screen. I was intimately aware of what events had already occurred in my life but it was the intensity that was so real. I even knew her name."

Finally, after a few minutes of thoughtful silence Shirley spoke. "Well, it looks like you've been experiencing each life in sequence. First Scotland, then Florence and now World War II in France. I'd say, it's time for a haircut and some make-up."

Clara shook her head and gave her a comic glare. "What?!"

Shirley laughed. "Think about it. The message from your grandfather was that it was *his* turn to find you. What if you misunderstood him and he wasn't talking about himself? What if he was telling you that it was Hamish's turn to find you?"

Clara knitted her eyebrows a little confused.

"Well? You want to be ready, don't you? You don't have to go crazy, but a nice haircut and a little mascara and some nice clothes would go a long way."

She shook her head. "I'm not following you."

Shirley tutted. "This isn't rocket science dear. Your next encounter could be *him*!" Her eyes widened to make her point. "Do you really want to look frumpy when you actually meet your soul mate? I don't think so."

When Clara looked somewhat convinced, Shirley pushed a little harder. "Tell you what, we'll book you in at my stylist for today so you don't change your mind."

"I can't today. I'll do it Wednesday. I've got boxes of books to unpack, price and shelve. Besides, by Wednesday my hair will be dirty, I'll be feeling rather frumpy and be ready for a change."

"Then tell you what, I'll book you for Wednesday, and pay for it – my treat, so I know for sure that you'll do it. Do we have an agreement young lady?"

Clara responded with a crooked grin. "We do."

CHAPTER TWENTY-THREE

By Wednesday night Clara was all a flutter. She had let the hairdresser choose the style that would suit her face, and although the cut looked fabulous, she was self-conscious about the new look. Gone was the old ponytail, fashionably replaced with a messy medium-length bob with highlights. What would Robert think? *Why did she even care what he thought?* To celebrate her new look, she had even bought a powder-blue cashmere sweater worth far more money than she would normally pay, but it was comfortable, which ticked her box, and was chic, which ticked Shirley's. After applying some mascara, she was even more anxious. What if he thought that she was doing all of this for him? *Was she?*

Shirley arrived at the bookshop early as usual and the wide smile on her face said it all. "You look fabulous! That bob is the perfect cut and I love the highlights!"

"Thanks. I just told her to do what she thought would look nice and was easy to take care of."

"I told you she was a wizard. Seriously – you look amazing."

Clara looked a little funny at Shirley.

"What's wrong?"

"Nothing really. It's silly I guess, but I didn't know this hairstyle was called a 'bob' and the officer from my dream was named Bobby and now tonight Robert is coming. Do you think it's a sign?"

Shirley leaned forward as she wiped the tables upstairs. "My dear, whether it is or isn't, it's best to let the universe unfold in the way that it wants. The bottom line is that you'll look fabulous no matter what the universe throws at you. Now, let's get ready, shall we?"

A short time later, Bryan and Scott arrived with rave reviews for the new doo, as did the Four Musketeers and Edward Bronson, who simply winked and nodded his approval. Even Bethany, who arrived with her boyfriend in tow, said how much she loved it. By the time Robert and his mother had arrived she was almost feeling comfortable with the change. She felt lighter not just because of the lack of weight from her hair, but more of a lightness of spirit that she couldn't quite define. She was in the fridge getting the cream when they arrived, so when she turned around, she saw him looking at her, immediately miming that he liked her hair. She felt a familiar warmth come to her cheeks indicating a deep blush, and mouthed a thank you.

During the break, Robert walked towards her and smiled. "Love the new haircut. It suits you."

Her hand automatically touched her hair. "Thanks, I was over-due. How's your case coming along? Or am I allowed to ask that?"

"No, no it's fine. It's done actually and it turned out well enough for my client, so I'm pleased. That's why I was able to bring my mum tonight."

"Well, we're happy you could join us."

"It's different than I thought it would be."

"Different? How so?"

"Well to be honest, I wasn't too sure what to expect. My initial reason for coming was to make sure that my mum wouldn't be taken in with anything, you know, shady."

"You mean like giving us thousands of pounds and we'll give you messages from your loved one kind of thing."

"Exactly. I hope I didn't offend you. I felt better when she told me that she knew Shirley, but I still needed to make sure things were on the up and up. This is a very vulnerable time for her."

"No offence taken at all. That just makes you a good son, looking out for his mum. And what do you think now?"

"To be honest, it's interesting, but like anything I can't explain, I'll respectfully remain a healthy skeptic until I find an answer I'm comfortable with."

"Fair enough."

"That's not actually why I came over here to talk to you though."

Clara smiled. "Go on."

"I was wondering whether you were free for lunch sometime. Or, if that's too difficult with the shop, maybe dinner?"

She could feel herself stumble. "Well, gosh, thank you. That would be very nice. I'd like that. Dinner would be easier I guess, if that's okay."

"Yes, absolutely. Maybe next weekend then?"

"Yes, I'd like that."

Robert and Clara ended up meeting at a restaurant near his office in Bridgewater. Clara felt nervous in the skirt and sweater set that Shirley had insisted that she wear. The weather wasn't the best and she rationalized that she would be both comfortable and chic with what she had selected.

He was already there when she arrived and was shown to the table by the Maître d'. She had to admit that she felt rather special meeting a man that handsome for dinner. He was dressed in a suit and tie and when he saw her, he stood to give her a quick peck on the cheek.

"Have you been here long?"

"No, not at all. You look lovely by the way."

She felt awkward. "Thank you."

After they had settled on a bottle of red, he smiled. "I hope you like Mediterranean food. It's fantastic here."

"I do, at least I think I do. I've never been to the Mediterranean. Have you?"

"I've been to Greece a few times and Italy of course. My next trip will be to Spain – Barcelona and Madrid."

"How exciting. I'm afraid I've led a rather boring life compared to yours."

"I don't believe that for a minute. Or, maybe you're just saving it for a time when you'll appreciate it."

"That sounds like a more exciting answer so I'll run with that. How's your mother?"

"She's at home meditating away. I'm not sure it will do any good, but it keeps her happy and that's all that matters."

"You're not a meditator I take it."

"Well, I can't say it really fits in with a lawyer's way of thinking, but it's what she wants to do. We get to spend time together and I get to keep an eye on her to make sure she's not, you know, going too far into woo-woo land."

"Is that what you think we do?"

"No, no that's not what I meant at all. I mean at first that was my concern, but now, not at all."

"Well, I guess that's a bit of a relief. Why do you bother to come at all then?"

"Honestly?"

"Yes, of course."

"I thought you would have guessed by now. So, I could see you."

"Me!"

"Well yes, who else? Surely not Bethany."

"Gosh. That's very kind of you to say that."

"It's the truth. I thought that if we had dinner, we could get to know each other a little better."

"That sounds nice actually. You're the solicitor, how do you suggest we begin?"

"How about you start by asking me a question."

Clara tilted her head and knitted her brows in faux concentration. "Do you have any brothers or sisters?"

"No. I was an only child and thoroughly spoiled. And you?"

This was fun. "My parents died in a boat accident when I was three, so I was raised by my grandfather. I inherited the bookshop from him, which is a very long way around to say I am also an only child."

"I'm sorry to hear that. That makes sense then why the message you received that night was so poignant."

"Yes." She lowered her head and nodded. "He was mum/dad and friend all rolled up into one hug of a grandad."

"You must miss him very much."

"I do."

"I lost my father when I was very young so I don't remember him. My mother didn't remarry until I was in my teens. I'm afraid I didn't take the competition for her affection very well."

Just then, the waiter came over with two menus for them to peruse.

"Shall we look at what's on the menu?"

"Absolutely. Any recommendations?"

"Hmmm, if you like fish, you can't go wrong with the Greek-baked cod with lemon and garlic. It's delicious. Or the seafood Paella. And if you're adventurous, try the Moroccan vegetable tangine."

"Wow, everything sounds delicious. What are you having?"

"I'm going with the Swordfish with lemon parsley topping and some pita with humous and labneh for us to share."

"I may go with the Greek-baked cod as long as you share one bite of your swordfish."

"I can agree to that if you're willing to surrender a bite of cod."

Clara smiled and was surprised at how easy he made it to flirt with him. "Done."

"Okay, my turn to ask you a question. What kinds of things do you like to do?"

"Well I do own a bookshop, so I like to read. How about you?"

"Golf. I took it up a few years ago and a lot of my colleagues play. It goes with the territory I suppose. Have you ever tried?"

"No, can't say I have. I liked to go horseback riding when I was twelve, but I've never had the opportunity to try golf. I don't know if I would be any good at it."

"It's all about practice. If you like, you could always come out with me one day. You don't have to play, but you might enjoy just walking around in nature."

"Sounds like a nice way to get exercise. I'd like that."

"You know I really like that haircut on you. It really suits you. You look very pretty."

Clara's cheeks reddened as she brushed a lock of hair from her eyes.

He continued. "You know, I like that you're shy. Your different from the women I meet at work. Either they are so independent that they're intimidating, or they are the kind that want to sink their manicured claws into you."

Clara chuckled and looked down at her unpolished, uneven nails. "Well, no worries there. With the number of books that I have to unpack and shelve, I couldn't keep manicured nails if I tried."

"You know, oddly enough I find that a very attractive trait. How about you? No husband—presumably no boyfriend…"

"No boyfriend. I guess because I haven't met anyone who likes me for just me, and besides I own a bookshop. That takes up a lot of my time."

"Well, I understand that issue well enough. My work tends to take over my life and as you already know I'm not always available. For my mum that's fine, but it's a bit of a relationship killer. I like that you have your own thing."

The waiter returned and took their order; the evening whirled by in a blend of flirtatious banter, good food, comfortable atmosphere, wine and interesting conversation. It was no surprise when at the end of their evening, he reached across and clasped her hand in his. "Perhaps we could do this again?"

She didn't hesitate. "I'd like that."

When they were outside, he walked her to her car, opened her car door and gave her a gentle, warm kiss.

"Would tomorrow be too soon to call for a second date?"

She grinned in spite of herself. "I look forward to it."

CHAPTER TWENTY-FOUR

*B*y 9:00 a.m. the next morning, Clara was at the bookshop. By 9:30 a.m. Shirley had already texted asking how her date had gone. Clara promptly replied for her to come over for tea in half an hour and she'd share. Shirley was there in ten.

"So? Tell me… I can't wait. Shag, marry or kill?"

Clara giggled. "Definitely shag and possibly marry. I had a nice time."

"And any second dates planned?"

"Well, he did ask if today would be too soon to call."

Shirley, cocked her head and raised her eyebrows. "That's a marry my friend."

"Shirley, you're incorrigible. We've only had one date."

"Well, he's not a kill, and who knows what the future may hold. I've got a client in an hour so I've got to scoot, but let me know when you're going out again. I'm reliving my youthful romances vicariously through you."

"Your Dave is probably one of the most romantic men I've ever met, so you're certainly not lacking in that department."

Shirley chuckled. "You're right there, love. He is indeed, but call me anyway and we'll chalk it up to me just being nosy."

"The moment he calls…"

After Shirley left, Clara dove into a whirlwind of chores simply to keep her mind occupied. Whenever the phone rang, her heart would beat faster, which was frustrating because she was trying to practice being cavalier about the whole dating thing. How would she ever get through this? A few customers came in, which helped her to focus on work, and by noon she was seriously considering dusting.

Finally, Robert called just as he said he would, but not until mid-afternoon, which had given Clara enough time to second guess herself and wonder whether he would actually call or not. He apologized saying that he had been caught up in court all day, to which Clara replied that it wasn't a problem at all because she had been busy all day with customers. She hadn't, but it made her feel a bit more independent and a woman of the world, of which of course she wasn't. His telephone voice was deep, smooth and silky. "I was thinking that maybe we could see a movie on Saturday night. Maybe go for a pint afterwards?"

Clara was taken aback. A handsome man not only wanted a second date, but it wasn't hard to figure out that a movie and a pint afterwards was the perfect prelude to a shag afterwards. *God, how long had it been?*

She didn't have to think any further. "Sounds perfect."

After they had agreed on the when and how, she hung up the phone, mentally reminding herself that by Saturday she would need to buy a new toothbrush, new underwear, shave her legs and clean the house. She calculated that because he was going to pick her up from her home that one of two things would happen. Either he would stay at her cottage or she would stay at his place after the pub, so it was best to be prepared either way. She confirmed her thoughts and strategy with Shirley who immediately dove into what she should wear.

By Saturday, Clara was a bag of nerves and worked off her tension by cleaning, polishing, sweeping, dusting and rearranging anything in sight, until the cottage looked like something out of

House & Home. The last two hours she would use to take a shower and get herself ready, crossed-checked by Shirley, who wanted pictures sent of the final effect they had agreed on—chic but casual.

By the time he arrived at 7:00 p.m., Clara had already run to the loo at least seventeen times, checked her make-up another six, double-checked her bedroom for anything that didn't say "goddess", and filled Lucy's bowl to the max (just in case). She answered the door in black jeans and a casual-but-nice red light-knit sweater, pearl earrings and a bracelet, an accessory item that Shirley insisted she wear to "feminize her look". Clara took one look at him and wondered how handsome men seemed to wear whatever they wanted and look incredibly sexy. Even his casual we're-just-going-to-a-movie look, looked expensive. He was dressed in pressed jeans that fit his slim physique, a casual blue shirt and a black jacket that somehow made him look like he just stepped off the cover of GQ. She immediately wondered whether or not she looked okay.

"Hey. You look nice. Are you ready?"

There was that relaxed, smooth voice again. Too late for changes now. "Yes, absolutely. Let me grab my purse and jacket and lock-up."

As they drove into the city, Robert suggested they see, "All is True", a biopic about William Shakespeare in his retirement years, a film that Clara had wanted to see anyway.

"Do you fancy a quick pint before we go in? Then we can grab another later on with some nibbles if you're up to it."

"Sounds perfect."

The evening flowed easily, the movie was sweet, sentimental and likeable, the conversations were comfortable, and he was attentive throughout the evening. He opened doors for her—a gentlemanly gesture that she found charming, and when the youthful, bouncy waitress arrived and flirted, he didn't respond (she scored him extra points for that).

The two pints they enjoyed later, were followed by some

laughs over previous date disasters. Clara's claim to her all-time worst date scenario was a blind date set up by a school chum. She had met the guy, as arranged, at a restaurant that he frequented. He seemed nice at first and suggested that because he knew the restaurant well, he would order. She was happy to comply. However, when the meal was brought to the table, what she realized was that he had ordered one meal for one person, to which he proceeded to share half in an extra plate. To add insult to injury, he spent the entire time talking non-stop about his previous girlfriend and their wonderful daily sex life—in detail.

Clara took a drink. "I just remember sitting there thinking. One. Why would my friend think this guy and I were compatible? And two. How can I get out of here as soon as possible?"

Robert shook his head. "What a wanker. My worst date was in college and the same scenario; I was set up by friends. I picked her up from her parent's home and we went to a pub just to have a few drinks and talk, but she didn't stop knocking them back. I was driving so I was watching my alcohol intake and couldn't get her to stop. By the end of the night she was doing multiple shots of Sex-on-the-Beach, by herself. She got so blotto that I didn't know what to do with her, so I took her home, propped her up against the front door and rang the doorbell several times. When I heard her father yelling, I took off not wanting to explain to him why his daughter was so drunk. In my defense though, after I drove off, I waited a few minutes down the road, then drove by again to make sure she was safely inside. She was, and I avoided ever seeing her again."

They told a few more stories and had a few more laughs before Robert downed the rest of his beer and suggested that they call it a night. It was 12:30 a.m., and the moment where the evening would either continue or end.

In the car, he proceeded to drive away from town and towards Butleigh. They drove without speaking, preferring to enjoy the smooth, jazzy music of Van Morrison. When he finally pulled up to her cottage, she wasn't sure what she should do. She broke the silence first. "Thank you for the evening. I really enjoyed myself...again."

"I did as well."

He then proceeded to get out of the car, walked over to her side and opened the door. Taking her hand, he helped her out and walked her to the front door.

Clara's mind was racing. *Should she invite him in? What should she do? What should she do? What should she do?*

Then in one perfect motion, he leaned in, lifted her chin and kissed her long and deeply.

As her question melted into a resounding yes, he looked into her eyes and smiled. "You know, I was wondering if you'd want to join me on Sunday. I have a golf game in the morning with my work colleagues and then everyone's coming over for a barbeque in the evening. It would be nice if you could join us. Meet some of my friends and their wives...maybe stay over?"

There was no question. "I'd like that."

They kissed once more before she unlocked her door and turned to look at him. "Thank you. I had fun tonight, Robert."

"I did too. See you Sunday." He leaned in and whispered in her ear. "And bring your toothbrush."

Once inside, Clara leaned her back against the door and closed her eyes. *Shag, marry or kill?* As Lucy loudly meowed her welcome home, Clara picked up her cat and gave her a kiss on the nose. "Shag, Lucy...definitely shag, then marry."

CHAPTER TWENTY-FIVE

*J*t was agreed she would drive to his place on Sunday after the golf game, but before anyone arrived, in order for her to help prepare dinner. It was a barbeque, so he would be taking over the grill, and after her afternoon with Susan, she felt confident she would at least be able to cut vegetables for a salad. Her only concern was meeting his friends. Would they like her? Would she like them? Would she fit in? Did they all play golf? Would she have to?

Over tea on Saturday, Shirley, who had played a few times, explained how it was more than just hitting a ball in a straight line, but Clara couldn't even feign interest with her friend.

"Walk me through this again. Why is this a fun thing to do?"

"It's not for everyone I admit, but when you are finally able to hit the ball far and straight enough, there is an attraction to the game. Besides, it's a nice way to spend time with friends. I'll warn you though, if he's into golf you'll need to either join him or enjoy being a golf widow."

"A golf 'widow'? That's really a thing?"

"It's definitely a thing, and if you two are an item, it's only a matter of time before he'll ask you to join him on the course."

"Thankfully I have a bookshop to run. I am nervous though about meeting his friends and then you know, afterwards…"

"Well, you're on your own in that department, but he does sound like a gentleman, so I'm sure you'll enjoy yourself. As for his friends, why in heavens would they not like you?" Shirley stood and patted her hand. "You're lovely and you'll have a wonderful time. And don't forget to wear the outfit we decided on! Give me a call when you're back home and you can tell me all the sordid details."

~

Clara arrived at Hamlet Wharf in Taunton, a forty-minute drive via the A361, around 2:30pm. She was impressed that he had travelled that far just to take her to a movie and back home again. His "home", was an apartment in a posh riverside development surrounded by well-manicured gardens, situated next to the river, and protected by large ornate security gates. When he mentioned he *just* had a three-bedroom flat, this was not at all what she envisioned. This was a whole level above "just".

After parking her car in the visitor's section, she was buzzed in and followed his instructions to his ground floor flat. She held on tightly to the bottle of wine she had brought (a little nod to Susan's chef rules), shifted her tote-style purse on her shoulder, took a deep breath and knocked on the door. He answered immediately and with a big hug welcomed her in. His apartment was, in a word, sophisticated. Manly. Immaculate and white. Very white. This was Robert at home, and everything was in its place, but she liked that, didn't she?

"Here, let me take that wine and come on in. How was the drive?"

"Lovely actually. The weather was nice, so it made the drive pleasant."

"Let me show you around. You can tuck your purse away in the spare room if you like."

She must have looked a little confused, because he smiled and added, "Or mine if you'd prefer."

She could feel herself blushing, and to cover it up remarked upon the unobstructed view of the waterway from his, not-a-streak-on-them, windows in the living room. "I love an open concept."

(She didn't.) "Is that the River Tone?"

"It is. There's a nice private patio garden if you'd like to sit outside and have a drink later."

"I'd love to."

His style was clean and crisp. His sofa set white, expensive, yet comfortable. Built-in storage was everywhere, but Clara was willing to bet most of the cupboards were empty. A single small golf trophy was displayed on his fireplace mantle, but slightly to the side so as to not interfere with a massive flat screen, while two floor-to-ceiling shelves contained row after row of thick reference-type books, perfectly aligned like soldiers at attention. On a side table was a picture of his mother and he at some kind of a formal event framed in silver. On the far end of what was an extremely spacious room, was a sleek dining table for eight and an immaculate kitchen. Modern in design, it was clean and white with black marble countertops. The cooking area was well-fitted with new appliances and a large island but bare of any colour or personal touches. Clara didn't cook, but even her kitchen never looked this tidy. Was he really expecting guests?

Putting his hand on the small of her back, he ushered her down the hall to continue the tour and nodded his head to the left. "I use this as an office when I need to work from home."

Clara poked her head through the door and eyed another, generously-sized room with a very organized polished mahogany desk and a large soft leather chair. One full wall was covered in shelves, more reference books and more built-in storage. The window and the desk faced the river, and she could well-imagine how peaceful it would be to work out of that office.

He carried on down the hall, with her following, pointing out that to the left was a spare room (nicely done up she noted). And finally, at the end of the hall, he opened the door to the master bedroom. She gasped. It was pure understated elegance and easily the size of two rooms put together. A huge contemporary grey bed took centre stage and was loaded with stylish pillows in various shades and patterns of black, greys and white. (Clara's first thought was that it literally cried out to fall backwards on.) The walls, in contrast to the white of everywhere else, were a deep and stunning grey. Hardwood floors accented the high ceilings and large patio doors faced the River Tone. Two cozy chairs sat by the doors, begging to be sat and read in, but what made her gasp was the large white Victorian fireplace feature that faced the bed, topped with a large flat screen TV, and lit by wall lights. This is what made the room a showstopper.

"It's like a 5-star hotel!"

"I like it. I had Deborah, my colleague's wife, design it for me. She'll be here tonight as a matter of fact." He nodded to a chair. "You can put your bag over there if you like."

They spent the next few hours sipping wine and chatting as he prepared some kind of barbeque sauce and placed chicken and steaks in large freezer bags to marinate. While he was busy with the main part of the meal, she was required to chop vegetables for a salad and thankfully not expected to create a gourmet dressing.

As he refilled her glass he smiled and gave her a little peck on her cheek. "I'm glad you're here. My friends have been asking when they were going to be graced with your presence."

"You've told them about me?"

"Of course. The girls are quite curious as to who has caught my eye."

"Well, I hope they're not disappointed."

"I'm sure you'll all get along like a house on fire. I'll barely be able to sneak in a kiss."

Clara grinned, stood on her toes and kissed him on his nose. "There's always time to sneak in a kiss."

Robert grabbed her by her waist and pressed his mouth to her ear. "Maybe we should just cancel my company for tonight?"

Unfortunately, before she and her beating heart could fire back anything remotely flirtatious and saucy, the doorbell rang.

As they gathered in the living room, she was introduced to the two couples, Mark and Joy, Deborah and Tony. Mark was a paunchy, slightly balding man in his early fifties and his girlfriend Joy, was a much younger, vivaciously busty blonde. Both were decked out in matching shades of kakis and turquoise golf shirts.

Next to be introduced was Tony and Deborah—*the bedroom designer*. Tony was a slender, much younger man than Mark, with a shock of red hair and freckles that seemed to cover his face and arms. Decked out in casual slacks and a black gold shirt, he had one of those open relaxed smiles and she liked him immediately. She did not, however, get the same vibe from his wife. A slender brunette, with not a hair out of place, she was clad in a simple spring dress that showed off deeply tanned legs, white leather sandals with gold accents and blue manicured toenails that matched her perfectly manicured nails. She was a pretty woman with a big smile and bright white teeth, and obviously trying far too hard. She gave a quick kiss to Robert's cheek and cooed, "Oh Robert, she's lovely!" Then turned and grabbed Clara's hands. "I can just tell already that you and I are going to be such best friends."

Clara, who felt like a deer in headlights, did her best to smile and assure Deborah that she must be right.

It didn't take long for the conversation to turn to golf and work, which meant that the next few hours were a blend of phrases like tee off, missed the can, birdie, carpets, four-jack and gimme. Robert did his best to include her in their conversations and she did her best to keep up, but by the time they were explaining to Joy about how she should "milk her grip" she was completely lost.

Robert then began the process of heating up the grill, and while Bonamassa played in the background, glasses were refilled, and the men joined him on the patio. Clara, after asking if he needed some help (he declined), prepared herself for the inevitable girl chat. She learned that Mark was divorced, but Joy assured her, for a very good reason. His ex-wife was a real bitch, costing him a lot of money. She was told how their grown children ignore her when she's done nothing wrong (obviously the ex's fault). How happy he is now, her new car (not in the colour she wanted though) and where in Tuscany they would be going next.

Deborah's conversational skills were no better. She was all-knowing about Robert and made sure that Clara knew she was an old-time friend and expert in all things Robert. "Robert is hopeless at choosing colours and fabrics. *Have you seen the bedroom?* Robert loves to sauna. He's such a good cook. That chateaubriand that he made last month was to die for. You'll love his mother, she's so sweet. Oh, you've met? *Really?*" She went on and on and on.

"Remember that time Robert, when the three of us found that restaurant in Greece, and Tony was so sick he had to stay in the hotel for two days? Do you golf, Clara? No? Well, we'll have to get you out on the course. Do you need me to toss the salad Robert? A bookstore? How quaint! We must do lunch sometime. Goodbyeeee, hug, hug, kiss, kiss. Lovely meeting you. I'm certain we'll be seeing much more of you."

Then suddenly it was over. Silence. They were gone. The dishes were stacked in the dishwasher, glasses were washed, the grill was scrubbed, the food was put away, and now Robert was holding out a small snifter of brandy. "So? What do you think of my friends? But before you say anything, they all thought you were fabulous. I know Joy is a bit of a sugar daddy girl, but she has a good heart and really seems to make Mark happy."

She did her best to give a facsimile of a genuine smile. "They all seem lovely."

"See? I told you you'd get along. For a while I thought we were going to have to kick Deborah out." He put down his brandy and wrapped his arms around Clara's. "I've been waiting to do this all night."

Tilting his head towards hers, he kissed her deeply. Once, then again and again, his breath quick and ragged as their physical passion grew from flicker to flame, to a torrid fire of immediate need and want. Forgotten brandy snifters were left on the table as he took her hand and led her to his room. She expected they would tear each other's clothes off, and he would slowly lower her to the bed as Hamish had done. He would love her so well that she would never want another. But this is not what happened. Instead, he gallantly suggested that she use the washroom before him. The shower was there, towels, shampoo etc. Clara did a double take. *Did she smell bad? What happened to ripping her clothes off?*

Clara felt a little weird as she climbed into the bed as he used the shower. Should she keep the towel around her? Wear a bra and panties, be naked? What was the best way to look sexy in this situation? She felt clueless. When he had finished his shower and brushed his teeth (presumably flossing as well) he came towards the bed in a towel. His skin glistened and the dim light accented his muscles. As he tore off his towel and slid under the covers, she was excited to note that the choice she made was the right one. Naked.

CHAPTER TWENTY-SIX

*T*he next few months flew by in a whirl. She and Robert had gone on several dates. They had stayed over at each other's home, but although she enjoyed his company, laughed at his jokes and looked forward to seeing him, their relationship lacked that deep spark that she had always hoped to find. She hated golf and hated watching it on TV more. His lawyer friends were nice enough, friendly enough, even Deborah calmed down after a while, but they weren't people that she would ever be friends with on her own. Deborah and Joy were far more glamourous than she felt she ever wanted to be.

As summer fell away and fall began, Clara needed Ellie, her occasional part-time shop-girl more and more, until it became the not-so-occasional Saturday, Sunday and evening shifts. At first, she was nervous about having anyone else but herself manage the shop, but from the moment Ellie walked through the doors Clara knew she would do. Besides, Shirley would be right next door should she encounter any issues. She wished all her decisions were this easy.

Lately she was feeling more and more that her and Robert's relationship was one of convenience rather than passion. By this time, she had heard all of his jokes and although he was nice, he felt "too" nice. They were two nice people in a nice relationship. In time they would have a nice marriage with nice children, in a nice neighbourhood. Is this what she was supposed to want? Was he her Hamish? Was she his Dorothea? It wasn't as if she wanted a bad boy or anything like that. She didn't. It was just that if their relationship was a flavour, she would have to say it was vanilla. Not a fancy French vanilla or the best vanilla you've ever tasted made from organic vanilla pods hand-picked in Madagascar by wood fairies in a secret vanilla forest hidden in a sacred mountain; just the regular old vanilla you'd find at a local convenience shop. What she wanted was an artisan vanilla with a bourbon-laced rocky road served in a red tartan bowl with sparklers. But this was the real world and she had never actually seen a red-tartan bowl. Maybe she was asking too much? Robert was solid, intelligent and a nice guy. He was everything she was supposed to want. He was the Hamish she dreamed up before the Robert she met.

One morning in November, Shirley popped in to let her know that she had heard from Susan. Good news. The work on Chamberlain House was on schedule and they were still on for the 1940's New Year's gala.

"Oh, that's wonderful news. I guess I should check with Robert to see if he has any plans."

"Well plans or no, you should be there. Besides, you promised Susan."

"I did, didn't I."

"Speaking of Robert, how is it going? You two are seeing a lot of each other."

"It's nice. He's nice."

"Hmmm. Nice. Tell you what, how about you and I spend a night in London. We'll take the train in, spend the afternoon shopping for our gala dresses, and have dinner in a nice restaurant. It'll be fun. And you can wow that Mr. Nice of yours on New Year's with a fabulous dress instead of the jeans you're constantly in."

Clara sighed. "Maybe your right. Last week he asked me if I even owned any dresses. He even made a suggestion that I go shopping with Deborah. I suppose it wouldn't hurt to freshen up my wardrobe, and I'd certainly rather do that with you. We can do some Christmas shopping as well."

~

That weekend, Clara and Shirley stepped off the train in London and went immediately to their hotel to check in and leave their overnight bags. Shirley was all for getting started right off the bat. "Right, I say we start on Bond Street for the dresses and then take a wander down Oxford towards Selfridges. Sound okay to you?"

"It sounds fine to me, although the shops on Bond may be a bit out of my price range."

"Don't you worry about that. We are here to have fun and part of that fun is to fatten our eyes with things we can't afford but look like we do. Now be a good girl and keep an eye out for movie stars. If we see George Clooney, you're on your own."

"You're incorrigible. You know that don't you."

As they sauntered down Bond Street, they wandered in and out of various shops with neither rhyme nor reason as to what they were actually looking for. After being closeted up with books all day, Clara had to admit that being out and about in noisy traffic and blustery fresh air was fun. They went into a few dress shops and Shirley tried on two that had caught her eye, but a quick look at the price tag caused her to exclaim to the shop girl that they just wouldn't suit. Passing by a café, they decided to take a break and have tea with a slice of cake. Clara chose the lemon sponge while Shirley settled for a raisin scone.

Taking a sip of her tea, Clara looked at Shirley. "Can I ask you something?"

"Of course, dear. Ask away."

"When you met Dave, did you know that he was the one?"

"Hmmm. I did and I didn't. It would be fairer to say that he knew right away, and I couldn't help but be convinced the more time we spent together. And then one day I just knew." Shirley put down her tea. "I'm guessing you're having second thoughts about Robert?"

"He's not the Hamish from my dreams, that much I know, but he's a nice man and I enjoy his company. But he's nice with everyone. He's as charming to other women as he is with me. I keep thinking that maybe I'm holding out for someone who doesn't exist in this lifetime. But if that's the case, what would have been the point of the past life remembrances?"

"Have you ever thought about what *you* want, Clara? So far, your life has been your bookshop and that's been it. Robert is your first really serious relationship and as you say, he's a nice man, but what is it you want? If I were to ask you to tell me what your perfect life looks like what would it be?"

"I don't know if I've ever really thought about it. I seem to slot myself into other people's story lines but have never written my own."

"Okay, then let's play a game. I'm going to ask you some questions and you're going to answer immediately—don't think about whether the answer is right or wrong. Understood?"

"Okay."

"City or village?"

"Village."

"Go out or stay in?"

"Stay in."

"Children?"

"Yes."

"Golfing or bicycling."

"Bicycling, but casual."

"Mexican beach vacation or exploring Scotland."

"Scotland any day."

"Chocolate or vanilla?"

"Hmmmm. Caramel swirl."

"Robert or Hamish?

"Hamish."

"Why?"

"Because I would never have to wonder whether it's me he loves. I saw it in his eyes. I felt it in his passion." Clara's face dropped. "Oh, my God, you know, Shirley, you have a point. When I think of being married, I think of us as a family, going cycling with the children, doing things together. Robert golfs a lot and sometimes I feel like he's disappointed that I have no interest in joining him. All of his friends' wives golf, but to be honest I'd rather stay home than have to walk the course with him. It's boring and I'm rubbish at swinging a club."

"Let's try this. If you had one secret wish that you would like to accomplish in your lifetime what would it be?"

"Honestly? For years I've had this children's book idea in my head."

"I bet that you would be very good at that. What's it about?"

"You'll laugh, but it's about a little orphan girl who's being raised by her grandfather in a magical bookstore and befriends two troublesome book fairies that live there. These fairies can be quite naughty, especially to people who have dirty hands or don't put a book back. Sometimes they like to organize the books the way that they like, which doesn't make sense to anyone else." Clara's eyes got bigger, and her voice became more excited as she continued. "For example, a book that's very suspenseful or intense would rather stand beside a more calming book. Or a book that's set in the city would like to be beside one that's set in the country or the seaside. Anyway, the book fairies cause quite a bit of chaos and everyone thinks that it's her grandfather getting too old to manage the store. The bank gets involved, and so does the rich snooty aunt, so the girl and the fairies have to work together to save the day."

"That's lovely, Clara and look at you! Your face lit right up when you were talking about it. Why haven't you written it?"

"I don't know, there's always one reason or another. Maybe

because I've never written anything in my life. And now, between Robert and the shop, I just don't have any time."

"Clara, if it's important to you then this is something you must make time for. And if it's important to you then it should be important to whoever you're with. Promise me that you will write this book. I have a very good feeling about it. If not for you, then for your grandfather."

Clara looked up, smiled and grabbed Shirley's hand. "Thanks, Shirl, you've been a huge help."

"You may be tired of hearing this, but I promised your grandfather that I would take care of you and I intend on doing just that. Now let's get back out there and find you the perfect dress for that New Year's gala."

As they continued down Bond Street, a dress shop across the street caught Clara's eye and she stopped briefly to make out what appeared to be a display of vintage-style dresses in the window. Shirley, noting her interest, suggested they go in and have a look around. Sure enough, as they got closer the dresses were entirely 1940's, V-neck, A-line, swing style. Her heart beat faster. Her perfect dress was here. She could feel it. The dress shop seemed oddly out of place beside the shiny larger retail giants with well-known names and bright lights. Even the older woman who approached them seemed from another time. Her hair was rolled up into a Victory roll, and her dress was straight from wartime London. Cara had the strangest feeling she was in a time warp.

"Hello, may I help you?"

"Yes, I'm looking for a nice dress to wear to a gala." (There was that word again, nice.)

Shirley interrupted. "She's not looking for nice, she's looking for fabulous."

The older woman took a good look at Clara's body shape and after a full minute of silence nodded her head, as if she had come to a conclusion. "I think I have just the dress you're looking for. There's only one and quite honestly, I've been waiting for the perfect person for it. Humour me and try it on?"

Shirley nodded on Clara's behalf and while the owner went into the back to retrieve the gown, Shirley took Clara's coat, bags and purse. The woman returned with a red gown in a clear garment bag and hung it in the changing room.

"Let me know when you're ready and I'll zip up the back for you. The larger mirrors are out here so you can come show your friend."

A few minutes later, Clara let the woman zip up the dress and as she escorted her out to see Shirley she already knew. The woman was talking to Shirley about the design but as Clara stared in the mirror, she only heard snippets of the conversation. "Strapless, red-draped tulle...hips in the French pannier style...very 1940's, and I must say it fits like it was made for you. I knew it would."

Shirley put her hands on her mouth and shook her head. "It looks fantastic. This is the dress, Clara. This is the dress. What do you think?"

As she stared into the mirror Clara heard Bobby's dying words. "We'll dance in our next life, won't we?"

"*In my red dress, I promise.*"

CHAPTER TWENTY-SEVEN

A week before she and Robert were going to his work Christmas party, Robert asked Clara to join him for dinner at a very expensive restaurant. Clara was certain that there could be only one reason for this, and it terrified her. He was going to propose. She was so worried that when Shirley came into the store the next day, she blurted out her fears before she could even say hello.

"Shirley, I need your help. You need to tell me what to do."

"What's happened love?"

"I think Robert's going to propose. He wants to take me out to dinner this Friday in a fancy restaurant. We're already going to his work party next week. What else could it be?"

Shirley raised an eyebrow. "Well, it certainly sounds like he's planning a romantic evening for two, so you could be right. How do you feel about it?"

"That's the thing. I don't know how I feel. He's everything I'm supposed to want, but I can't help feeling that I'm settling, which is stupid because if anything, he's the one who's settling, not me."

"Well now that's just not true. Anyone would be lucky to have someone like you. But if you feel this strongly, isn't that your answer?"

"I guess, but what if I'm wrong? Maybe nice is what I should want. What if I'm in love with a fairy tale? Or there's no such thing as love at first sight. Maybe there's no Hamish. Maybe I'm making the biggest mistake of my life by not marrying him."

"Or if you're agreeing to something you may not be ready for, that in itself is a very valid reason to say no, or not yet. If you're not ready to take the relationship to the next step, then say that and don't do it until you are."

Clara's shoulders relaxed with relief. "You're absolutely right Shirley and I feel comfortable with that answer. I love you, you're a genius."

On Friday Clara was fidgety all day. She was cranky with Mrs. Filer who couldn't remember the name of the book she wanted and grumbled when the post came late. Robert had arranged to pick her up at 7:00 p.m. and it was only 2:00 p.m. now. How was she supposed to cope over the next few hours? When she finally closed the shop, drove home, fed Lucy and got herself showered and dressed, she found herself ready with half an hour to spare. She paced. Rearranged her mother's china figurines, checked her appearance for the hundredth time and paced some more. Looking in her full-length mirror she questioned her choice of dresses, but Shirley had assured her that her new chic black one was the one to wear. She double-checked the manicure she just had done then put on another set of earrings, and then agreed that the first pair was better, until at long last, he arrived.

As she opened the door his face beamed. "Hey beautiful! Ready to go?"

Her heart skipped a beat seeing how handsome he looked in his suit and tie and for a brief moment she was confused. *Maybe she wanted to say yes?* "Absolutely. I'm looking forward to it."

The drive to the restaurant was casual and comfortable, each chatting about their week, and Clara found herself relaxing, that perhaps her fears were unfounded. Maybe she *should* marry him.

When they arrived at the restaurant they were escorted to their table by a crisp-collared Maître d', who handed them both a menu and asked if they would like to start with a drink. Robert nodded, then, always more confident in ordering than she was, requested an expensive Cabernet Sauvignon and then turned his attention back to Clara. While waiting for the wine, they discussed the menu and decided on the roast beef, confirmed the Christmas gift they had chosen for his mother and whether or not they would ever find the treasure on Oak Island until the waiter returned.

After a brief toast, Robert suddenly looked serious. "You must be wondering why I picked this restaurant."

"Well, it is rather posh."

"It is, but I wanted tonight to be special. Hopefully a celebration. But first there's something I need to discuss with you."

Clara's heart pounded and her mouth went dry. This was it. He was going to ask. What should she say? What should she do? Calming herself as best she could, she took a large sip of wine. "Okay."

He looked awkward and unsure of his words. *Did all men act this way at proposals?*

"It's to do with my work."

What? Clara was confused. On the one hand she had no choice but to admit that she felt relieved. This was not a proposal, but on the other hand, why was he being so serious?

"I've been offered a promotion."

Clara's eyebrows knitted. "That's wonderful news, isn't it?"

"Yes, absolutely. It's wonderful news. It's just that they've asked me to take over the New York branch as a Senior Partner and the thing is, I've said yes."

"Oh!" Clara needed a moment to process this. "Well, you couldn't turn it down; it's such an incredible opportunity isn't it."

"Yes, it is. I just don't know where that leaves you and I and I needed to tell you before they announce it at the party next week."

"I can certainly see how that would have been awkward. When does this new position start?"

"Right after New Year's, but I'll need to be set up by then, so almost immediately actually."

"So now."

"Yes. I'll be back for Christmas of course. I was thinking though, that maybe you would consider joining me for New Year's. We could do it New York style—Times Square... Broadway plays...the whole nine yards. What do you say?"

"It sounds exciting of course but the thing is I've already committed myself...us actually...to the Chamberlain House gala."

"Well, that's easy enough to cancel considering the situation."

"Yes, of course it is, but I'm not so sure that I want to."

"You could come for a month. Maybe you'd even like it there."

"Robert, this is a lot to take in. I'm happy for you, I truly am, but it's a big decision. I don't know if I would ever be ready for a full diet of New York or bright lights or Broadway. It's just not me. I have a cat and I own a bookshop that I can't just shut down for a month."

"I thought you'd want to share this with me."

"Then you should have asked me my opinion first."

"Look, this isn't something I can say no to. It's not even something I want to say no to."

"Robert, I'm not asking you to. In fact, I don't want you to. If New York is the direction your career needs to go, then I am thrilled for your opportunity. It's just not my dream."

"I see. Where does that leave us then?"

"I don't know, Robert. Good friends?"

Robert was silent for a long minute and looked down. "Well, this celebration dinner is a bit of a bust."

"Not at all. I'm actually thrilled for you Robert. Truly I am.

Let's just take this one step at a time though. I'm proud of you so let's celebrate and drink a 'cheers' to your brilliant career and whatever New York success offers."

"You're a very special woman, Clara."

"You know, Robert, I'm finally beginning to think so as well."

∾

Christmas came and went. Clara and Robert spent it with his mother, who did her best to lighten the mood and keep the conversations going. She had already made plans to visit her son in the spring in the US and was busy fussing about how much he was going to be missed. It was clear that she felt Clara was making a big mistake but was no less polite and warm towards her. There wasn't a day where Clara didn't have mixed feelings about him going. *Who would she be when he left?* She looked down at her polished nails. Would she go back to old habits? She shrugged. Maybe not. She liked the different colours, so maybe she'd try some that were even more exciting. Maybe she'd write. She nodded her head. *Yeah, maybe she'd finally write about the book fairies. Get another cat. Sell the bookshop and travel. Why the hell not?*

Clara took Robert to the airport on the 27th of December at 11 a.m., kissed him on the cheek and sent him on his way. By 2 p.m., she was back in the bookstore serving customers and wondering yet again, whether she had made a mistake.

CHAPTER TWENTY-EIGHT

*B*y the 30th of December Clara was quite adamant that she was going to stay home for New Year's and called Shirley to tell her so. "I'm not going."

"You most certainly are."

"No, really I'm not. I won't be any fun. And I'll be all alone again. Maybe I should have gone to New York. Who else but me would say no to New York?"

"You said no to New York for all the right reasons. And you won't be alone, you'll be with us."

"Third wheel."

"I highly doubt you'll be the third wheel for very long in that dress."

Clara groaned. "I forgot about the dress. I don't even feel like wearing it now."

"Clara. I am going to have to pull rank on you. Your grandfather made me promise to keep an eye on you and that's just what I intend on doing. You, my dear, have no choice in the matter. Dave and I will be there tomorrow at noon to pick you up and you'd better be ready young lady—with the red dress in tow. Understood?"

Clara rolled her eyes and chuckled. "Yes, ma'am. Understood ma'am. I'll be ready to deploy at 12:00 hours."

"Perfect. At ease, and we'll see you soon."

Shirley and Dave were there promptly at noon the next day, but before Dave popped her suitcase in the trunk, Shirley went over Clara's list of things to bring. "You've brought the red dress and shoes?"

"Yes."

"Make-up?"

"Yes."

"That nice light blue cashmere sweater of yours?"

"No. But I brought my red one."

"Not nice enough. Go get the blue one and put it in your suitcase."

"But the red one is comfortable."

Shirley stared her down. "Then wear it when you are cleaning the house. Not when you are on a grand estate."

"But..."

"No buts...bring the red one if you must but pack that lovely blue one. It shows off your eyes."

"I feel like you're my mother."

"Perfect, because that's exactly the tone I'm going for right now."

Clara headed off to her bedroom and returned with the sweater in hand. "Happy?"

"Absolutely. Off we go. Chop, chop, we've got a long drive ahead of us."

They arrived around 2:30 p.m. in the afternoon and were greeted at the reception desk by a pretty young lady in her twenties dressed in a traditional Army Nurse Corp uniform, complete with cap and red lipstick.

The renovations were absolutely stunning and done to a very high standard. Every direction they looked had received the utmost care and attention of qualified tradesmen. The hand-carved wooden staircase gleamed, cornices had been expertly repaired, and the newly painted walls had all been exquisitely and sympathetically restored to their original Georgian splendor. Chamberlain House was a gem. To set the mood, all the décor was centred around World War II memorabilia with fairy lights everywhere.. A wartime poster framed and hung on the wall showed a little boy with a wooden sword as a soldier held him back. The caption stated, "Leave Hitler to me Sonny—You ought to be out of London." Another one near the reception desk exclaimed "Britain shall not burn!"

The young lady looked up from her computer. "Ah, Mr. and Mrs. Forde, Clara Bennet and Robert Evans is that correct?"

Clara opened her mouth to speak but Dave was already replying. "Mr. Evans is not able to make it so it will be just Clara for the weekend."

"Well, I'm sorry he won't be joining us. It's promising to be quite the gala. Susan wanted to greet you personally, but she's been quite busy with last minute details. I'll set you up with your rooms and keys. Drinks will start around 6:00 p.m., so you've got plenty of time to relax before the party starts."

"Thank you."

As they reached their respective rooms, Dave turned to Shirley and stretched. "You know I could use a bit of a kip."

She smiled back at him and placed her hand on his shoulder. "And I could use a shower. Clara?"

"I think I might have a bit of a walk and get some fresh air."

"Should we meet around 6:00 p.m. then? I'll give you a knock on your door when we're ready and we can all go down together."

"Perfect."

Clara opened her door and held her breath. The room was no

less beautiful than the first time she had seen it. The faded light green panels were now an eggshell blue and the chipped white trim and crown moldings had obviously been repaired and repainted. The chandelier had been noticeably cleaned, and the carved oak four poster bed had a canopy above. The room, combined with the thick white duvet and bolstered pillows, created a very a pretty picture, and she snapped one with her phone to remind her for later.

She hung up her dress and unpacked her things then sauntered over to the window to watch a man emptying boxes from the back of a Honda civic. She squinted. There was something instantly familiar about him that made her wonder at first if it was Robert, but at second glance she noticed that his hair was too dark, and she dismissed the idea. Besides, he was dressed in a T-shirt, black leather jacket and jeans, hardly Robert's style. It was definitely time for a walk.

Bundling herself up she headed down the stairs and out the front door. The car and the man were just leaving but she did get a quick glimpse of a handsome face. *Not bad for the help.* Remembering the layout of the grounds she decided to walk towards the terrace at the rear of the house and climbed down a few steps to the water meadows and a small brook where swans peacefully floated by. So, here she was yet again, another New Year's Eve —alone.

She looked around and took in a deep breath of fresh air. Why had she let Shirley talk her into coming here? She could be at home right now in her pyjamas making decisions as to what book to read or what movie to watch, while Lucy happily snuggled up on her lap. She had to admit, she felt sad about Robert leaving. She missed his company. After all, were his jokes really that bad? And isn't that what you did when you were a couple? Put up with the little things?

A pair of swans glided by in unison, and she watched them intently. Her Grandad had told her once, how swans form monogamous bonds that last for many years, and in many times for life.

Their loyalty was so storied that the image of two swans swimming, their necks entwined in the shape of a heart had become a universal symbol of love. Maybe in her next life she would be a swan.

She thought about Hamish, about her past life memories of Florence, of being a combat nurse and about the blue leather book. Lastly, she thought about Robert. What did all of this mean to Clara Bennet in the here and now? In Scotland, Thea knew her own heart and although she couldn't follow it and be with Hamish, she had certainly found her one true love—her soul mate. Her leap away from him, from love, saved his, as the concussion ended hers.

In Florence, Klara had followed her career but not her heart and later regretted some of the decisions she had made. Would she have become a doctor though had she married Michael Chamberlain? Clara pondered this for a few moments while watching the swans. Not likely. In England she would have been expected to fit into Victorian society, have several children, and through no fault of his own, Michael's life would have swallowed hers whole, completely changing her life's direction. And by doing that, how would that have impacted other people's lives or young girls' dreams of being something more because of what Klara had already accomplished?

In World War II, her life had counted for something. What she did was important. It had meaning. She had not found love till the end, but she had found love nonetheless and they died together. So, what was her lesson for the here and now? What was her unfinished business?

Looking down at her manicured nails she thought about how Robert's life had little by little become hers. The truth was that Clara had never explored what *she* wanted, let alone pursued it with a passion. She loved the bookstore because it was familiar. It was her past, her memories, but it was never really a choice that she had made for herself. It was the road easily followed, just as Robert was a path easily taken. She had been slowly turning into someone who fitted into his life. She shook her head. Before his job offer in New York, she had even been considering golf lessons for God sakes. Shirley was right, she needed to figure out what she wanted. She spent several more minutes just staring at the water, watching the soft undulating current, the peaceful surroundings, and toyed with the idea of selling the bookshop. Who would she be without it? An author? A traveller?

She looked at the time on her phone and noticed it was after four, leaving her just enough time to have a bath and get ready. Taking one last look at the swans, she headed back to her room.

CHAPTER TWENTY-NINE

*C*lara checked herself one last time in the mirror before opening the door to Shirley and Dave. She had done her hair in smooth finger waves on top, but below had left it loose and wavy, and brushed away from her face. The princess bodice required her to wear a strapless bra with a low back, making her feel a little self-conscious, but oddly excited. She slipped on her shoes and grabbed a small sequined clutch from the dresser and opened the door. "Oh, my goodness you two look fabulous!"

Dave struck a "007" pose and looked very dapper in a black suit, crisp white shirt and black bowtie, while Shirley's gown was floor-length and lightly gathered with beading at the neckline. On top, she wore a short dinner jacket, beaded all along the front with square shoulder pads. Her hair was rolled into a classic 1940's half up, half down style.

Dave circled his finger towards Clara as she giggled and did a girlish twirl. Dave chuffed, "I'll be the envy of all the men here tonight with you two on my arm. I'll be fighting them off!"

Shirley gave Clara a quick wink and a hug. "He's right you know. You look stunning!"

Clara blushed. She had to admit that dressing up made her feel special.

Dave put an arm out for both of the ladies. "Shall we have a drink my lovelies?"

As they took the stairs down to the main area, the buzz of voices began to filter through the halls. A small group of people were gathered at the base of the stairs and as Clara descended, several of the men looked up with an admiring glance. She blushed and smiled in appreciation. How she wished Robert was here to see her. In a large reception room, now designated as a bar area, there was a crowd of at least one hundred people, all dressed in their best 1940's fashion. A man in a slick black suit played a soft melody at a grand piano while waiters in tails glided around the room with trays of champagne. Clara, Shirley and Dave each took a glass and gave a brief cheers to each other. Shirley and Clara kept a look out for Susan, who suddenly appeared by their side. Channelling her inner film star, Susan looked stunning in a classic mossy green sequined gown with a cinched in waist and long fuchsia gloves covered in bangles.

"My goodness, don't you all look wonderful!" She looked around her. "So, what do you think of the old lady now?"

Dave chuckled. "I hope you're referring to the house because I don't see any old ladies here."

Susan playfully smacked his arm. "The house of course! She looks wonderful, doesn't she?" There was obvious pride in her voice, and rightfully so.

Dave nodded. "She does indeed. You've done an amazing job. My hats off to you."

"Well, it wasn't just me. Shay deserves most of the praise. He's tireless that boy. As a matter of fact, tonight, I'm under strict orders to do nothing but enjoy myself. He's the one in charge. Have you met him yet?" Looking around, she continued. "I know he's around here somewhere."

Clara smiled. "No, but I can imagine he's quite busy."

Susan looked back at Clara and smiled. "My dear, you look gorgeous tonight. An absolute stunner. And where is this young man of yours so I can meet him?"

Clara put on a brave face. "He wasn't able to make it I'm afraid."

"On New Year's Eve? Why ever not? I hope he's not ill?"

"No, not at all. He's taken on a new position in New York."

"Really? Well, that's rather sudden isn't it?" She linked her arm into Clara's. "Listen, you and I are going to have a good chinwag this weekend. For tonight though, you're to have some fun and that's an order. Shay's on his own tonight too and there's plenty of men to dance with. With that dress, your dance card will be full in no time. Now, if you excuse me, I've got to say some hellos. Drink up—enjoy."

The threesome chatted amiably with their champagne and played guessing games as to the occupations of the guests. A chubby older man was likely the Mayor. An older matronly woman in a dinner jacket decorated with beads was probably a barrister's wife, and a spindly old woman dripping in sequins, in what had to be a vintage gown, was probably a distant cousin to the Queen.

A short time later the group was escorted into the lavishly decorated ballroom with a series of magnificent windows that spanned the length of the first floor. The grand crystal chandeliers sparkled.

There were a number of tables laid out in white linen, fine china, crystal, bouquets of flowers and subtle fairy lights every-where. The effect was absolutely magical. They were seated at a table with three other people, an older couple with an even older woman, who smiled back politely. The gentleman introduced himself as Simon and his wife Dee, whose cheeks glowed a rosy apple red. "And this young lady," pointing to the much older woman "is our Great-Aunt Maggie."

Maggie, who was sitting next to Clara, patted her shoulder and chuckled. Her thick brogue clearly giving her away as a Scot. "He's such a tease that boy."

They all chatted politely for a while. Dave and Simon shared a few laughs at their wives' expense, while retorts from both women brought gales of laughter from all.

Clara leaned towards Maggie and asked where she was from in Scotland.

"Ach, ye would nae have heard of it love. It's a small village outside of Edinburgh."

"I'm sure it must be beautiful there."

"Oh, aye," she said in a thin treble voice. "It used to be lovely countryside, but it's all built up now isn't it? Hamish and I used to play around the castle ruins when we were younger."

Clara's heart did a double thump. "Did you say Hamish?"

"Aye, dear. Hamish was Shay's great-grandfather and my brother. Lovely man—bless him. Very much like our grandfather before him I can tell you. Broke my heart when he died."

"I'm sure you must miss him."

"Well, that's the curse of living so long, isn't it? Mind, my memories are still sound so that's something. Hamish and I, we were always looking out for an adventure, maybe even a ghost or two. We never actually did, but there was one night that we were sure we saw something. To this day, I don't know what it was, but it scared the bejesus out of us."

"What castle was it?"

"Well dear, it been only ruins since I was a wee child but it was called Dunbrae Castle in its day."

Clara paled. "Dunbrae?"

"Aye. They say the Earl's daughter, Dorothea, was madly in love with a servant, as he was with her, but it was not to be. On Hogmanay, the night before her ill-fated wedding to the Marquis, she mysteriously died. After her death, when the Marquis found out that she and the servant had lain together, he had him murdered. It was rumoured the two lovers promised to find each other again in another lifetime and I believe that to be true. My own granny used to say that there's only one night of the year they would find each other – New Year's Eve, the night she died."

Clara's face paled and her hands shook as she took a sip of wine. The old woman continued.

"Silly ghost story, I know, but I think of it every New Years' Eve, and I always like to think she found her true love in the end."

Clara gave a weak smile and looked over towards Shirley to catch her eye, but she was deeply engaged in a conversation with the other guests. "I'm so sorry, but I'm afraid you'll need to excuse me for a minute."

"Of course, dear. I hope my ghost story didn't upset you."

"No, not at all." Clara stood up feeling a little light-headed as she made her way to the ladies' room. The whole idea was absurd, but it had really shaken her up. How was this possible? Taking a few minutes to calm herself down, she tried to rationalize this as a wild coincidence and slowly walked back to the gala lost in her own thoughts. As she neared the ballroom, she could hear her Grandad's favourite song, "*It Had to be You*", start to play, and more than ever she felt alone. As she entered the room and saw all the couples dancing, her heart sank. Why wasn't she in New York? "*... Why do I do just as you say?*"

Suddenly a man's voice came from behind. "There you are! I've been looking everywhere for the beautiful woman in the red dress. I thought that you were like Cinderella and had escaped."

"*It must have been that something that lovers call 'fate'...*"

She turned to see a handsome face looking back at her. It was the man she had seen earlier from her window, but there was something in his eyes that seemed familiar, and her breath stopped. His dark, reddish-brown hair framed a strong jawline, and deep brown eyes drew her into his world. And in that moment, Clara knew in her soul that she already knew him, that she already loved him and that she desperately needed to see him again.

"*It had to be you, it had to be you...*"

He smiled, took a step forward and held out his hand. "Would you like to dance?"

She could barely speak, her eyes intently on his. "I would love to, thank you."

"I'm Shay by the way. Well, Hamish, really, but my mother called me Shay as a child because my father was a Hamish as well. The nickname stuck."

"Shay? Then you're Susan's son. I know your mother... I'm Clara."

"You're *that* Clara. She's been dying for me to meet you. You know, you'll think I'm crazy, Clara, but I feel like I've met you before."

In that magical moment everyone else seemed to disappear. There was just the two of them, the air heavily weighted with a knowing, a recognition. She stared into his familiar brown eyes. "I don't think you're crazy at all."

"I can't explain it. I saw you standing there in that red dress and I just knew I had to come over to meet you and ask you to dance."

"*For nobody else gave me a thrill...*"

Suddenly they were both quiet and had the overwhelming sense that they both had all the time they needed to get to know one another.

"*... with all your faults I love you still...*"

Time seemed to stand still as Clara rested her cheek on his suit lapel and inhaled the scent of his cologne against his skin. She had a million sensations running through her but the strongest was that her heart had finally found a home.

He in turn, drank in the perfume of her hair in the knowing that he had finally found the woman he was meant to be with.

As the two danced, Shirley and Susan watched on from the sidelines. Shirley raised her champagne glass in a toast. "I think you were right."

Susan nodded and laughed. "I'm thinking a June wedding."

"*It had to be you, wonderful you, it had to be you.*"

CHAPTER THIRTY

Five Years Later,
Chamberlain House, Oxfordshire.
31ˢᵗ December

The morning started as it always did, in the kitchen, and as usual, when Clara entered the room, she smiled at the scene before her. Susan and Molly were already at the family table, with Susan biting into a warm croissant and Molly picking the raisins out of her porridge and popping them into her three-year old mouth. Baskets of fresh herbs and vegetables were everywhere a flat surface would accommodate them. The kitchen help were busy getting started at the far end, one chopping away at something garlicky and the other with something green. Coffee and tea were already brewed, boiled eggs were being kept warm, and a variety of jams and jellies were spread across several silver trays. It was going to be a busy day.

Clara sat down beside her curly, red-headed daughter and kissed her on the nose, causing a little squeal of delight. "I thought I would find you here, Miss Molly."

"I made breakfast with Granny."

Clara looked over to Susan, her eyes sparkling.

"Did you really? Granny, is this true?"

Susan gave a nod and a wink. "She did, indeed. In fact, she made some for you and daddy as well."

Clara eyed the two obviously cold bowls of stiff porridge, devoid of any raisins. "Well, aren't you thoughtful, and you've taken out the raisins as well."

Molly looked up wide-eyed and smiled. "Uh, huh. They wanted me to."

"Did they? Well, daddy will be thrilled. I can't wait to taste it after my tea."

"Taste it now, Mummy."

"Can I have my tea first?"

"No. You need to eat your breakfast now."

Stifling a giggle at her serious face, Clara took a spoonful and widened her eyes. "Hmmmmmm, this is the best porridge I have ever tasted."

Molly was obviously pleased. "Granny already ate hers, but she was full and couldn't eat it all, so I told her five bites."

Susan nodded in mock compliance, then looked up at Clara. "Shay up?"

"Yes, he'll be down in a minute." Turning to her toddler, Clara said, "Do you remember what happens tonight?"

Molly nodded. "We're having a party."

"That's right! And mummy's going to help granny today and daddy is going to be busy with the rest of the fairy lights."

"Can I have fairy lights?"

"Well, my love, I'll bet you that if you're a very good girl today and do what nanny says, daddy will put the very special fairy lights in your bedroom. Would you like that?"

Molly's curls bobbed away in excitement. "Mummy, will fairies come if we put up the lights? Like the ones in your book?"

"Well, not the naughty ones like in my book, but nicer ones

who leave rainbow kisses and unicorn dreams for good little girls."

Just then Shay, dressed in jeans and a sweatshirt, walked into the kitchen, grabbed a croissant and kissed them all on their heads. "Good morning, lovely ladies. Are we all ready for tonight?"

"Daddy, Mummy says you can put up some fairy lights in my bedroom; will you?"

"I will indeed, but only if you help me and show me where they should go. I'll need a big girl to help me with that part. In fact, that could be our special project before nanny comes. What do you say?"

Molly raised her arms in success. "Yes, yes!"

Shay then formally addressed his mother and wife. "Granny, Mummy, for the next hour my daughter and I are going to transform her room into a fairyland." He turned to Molly. "But first, my little fairy princess, I must have coffee."

"And your porridge."

Shay looked down at the cold bowl of porridge, back up at his daughter's eager face, then at Clara and his mother valiantly attempting to stifle their giggles. Then, with great fanfare, he picked up a spoon and comically ate the entire bowl with a look that confirmed to little Molly that it was the best porridge he had ever tasted in his life. Clara's heart was fit to burst. Never could she imagine that she could be so happy. She thought about where the last five years had taken her and her leap *to* love. Shirley had taken over the management of the bookshop, along with her niece Ellie, and with the help of another part-timer, and managed to do a very tidy business between the books and readings.

Clara's first novel, "The Book Fairies" was received with rave reviews, and a sequel was already well in the works. Susan was everything she could have possibly wanted in a mother. She was even there when Molly was born, as she would be again with their next one. Clara was blessed, her personal book filled to the brim with chapters of cooking, giggles, love and many, many hugs.

~

Later that evening, Clara checked herself in the mirror and smoothed down her dress. This year's theme was "Come as Who You Were", and she couldn't be more excited. She had to have her costume specially made from memory, but the expense was worth every penny. Tonight, she would wear a white satin gown with pink panelled sleeves and a matching petticoat. Her pearl eardrops and necklace framed her auburn hair, which was done up in curls, making her look every bit like the Earl's headstrong daughter. Tonight though, she would be wearing her dress for *him*.

After a little knock on the door, Susan poked her head through. "Just popping my head in to see if you need any help and to let you know that Shirley and Dave have arrived. Dave says he is positive he was 007 in a past life." As Clara turned around, Susan put her hands to her mouth. "Oh, my goodness, Clara – you're beautiful. Has Shay seen you yet?"

"No, I wanted it to be a surprise. After we put Molly to bed, I told him he had to get dressed on his own."

"I'm sure he'll manage. Well, you look stunning, that's all I can say. I'm off to get dressed myself. I'm crossing my fingers that no one else will be Marie Antoinette in a past life." Susan gave a quick glance to Clara's tummy. "Not too tight I hope."

Clara took a step forward and gave her a big hug. "Not yet, and I can't wait to surprise him."

After Susan had left, Clara took one last look in the mirror and crept down to her office/writer's den. Searching through the books on her shelf she found the one she wanted and pulled it forward. She held it close to her chest as she walked over to the much larger Chamberlain library and pulled on the heavy oak door. There was something that she needed to do. Something that needed to be returned to its rightful place.

As she entered the room, she took a deep breath and smiled. There it was, her favourite scent in the world—the enchanting aroma of old books and the echo of long-forgotten words span-

LOVE IS A LEAP

ning hundreds of years. She turned on a small lamp sitting on the desk that bathed the room in a soft yellowed light. To Clara, it had the magical effect of transforming the library to an earlier time and it never failed to warm her heart.

Holding the blue leather book in her one hand, she softly stroked the antique leather with the other and whispered the inscription she already knew by heart.

"My heart enchanted, has loved you through endless lifetimes before, and will search for you again, for a hundred lifetimes more..."

Soft footsteps interrupted her, and she turned to see her husband handsomely dressed as Professor Michael H. Chamberlain II in the doorway.

He stood and stared. "God, you're beautiful."

She could feel herself blushing and glowing with love as he entered the dimly lit room.

Standing behind her, he wrapped his strong arms around hers and rested his head on her shoulder. "Dorothea, I presume?"

Clara giggled. "Why Professor Chamberlain, how did you ever guess?"

"I had a feeling. Which is why..." Taking a step back, he retrieved something from his vest pocket. "I had this made for you." With both hands he held out a necklace with a silver locket crafted into a heart. "It's not near what you deserve, but I wanted you to know how much Molly and I love you."

After he had clasped it on around her neck, Clara turned to face him and with a contented breath, smiled and looked deeply into his eyes. "Well Professor Chamberlain, in seven-and-a-half months your heart will need to leave enough room for one more."

Shay beamed. "Really?"

Clara giggled. "Really, really."

He nodded to the blue leather book now sitting on the shelf and raised an eyebrow.

She grinned. "I wanted to put it back where it belonged,

187

Professor. It's done what it was always meant to do. For us to find each other."

Taking her hand in his, he continued the poem. *"In life after life, in age after age, I will find you and love you, from the past, to the present, through lifetimes evermore."*

She gave a contented sigh and softly kissed her husband, her Hamish, her Shay. Life was not about who she had been or who he had been. It was about being true to who they were now, living it to the best of their ability, perfect in their glorious imperfections and *that* was more than enough for Clara.

~

Don't miss out on your next favorite book!

Join the Satin Romance mailing list
www.satinromance.com/mail.html

THANK YOU FOR READING

~

Did you enjoy this book?

We invite you to leave a review at your favorite book site, such as Goodreads, Amazon, Barnes & Noble, etc.

DID YOU KNOW THAT LEAVING A REVIEW…

- Helps other readers find books they may enjoy.
- Gives you a chance to let your voice be heard.
- Gives authors recognition for their hard work.
- Doesn't have to be long. A sentence or two about why you liked the book will do.

ABOUT THE AUTHOR

Kate Riley is a professional business coach, facilitator, artist, and author of *The Last Cathar*, *The Greening of the Laurel,* and *Love is a Leap.* Having grown up in a haunted house, Kate started searching for her own answers to the unexplained at an early age, leading to a lifelong passion for anything to do with things esoteric. When she's not writing, she enjoys expanding her culinary talents accompanied with a nice glass of red wine, delving into the mysteries of Oak Island, and adding to her already out-of-control library.

As a seasoned traveler, Kate has been able to combine her wanderlust with first-hand research for her books, whether at Montségur in France, the streets of Florence in Italy, collecting information on the Knights Templar in Scotland, or sharing a Guinness with friends and family in a Dublin pub.

Kate is blessed with five talented grandchildren, 3 rescue cats, and her beloved canine protector, Stoker. She currently lives in Innisfil ON.

www.katerileybooks.com

 facebook.com/Kate-Riley-1704834233070805